Presentiment of Death . . .

They were coming to another cave, opening out and away from the madness of Lucifer Cove. Just as she stepped into the larger cave, a shadow crossed her face. She closed her eyes for a moment. When she opened them, Marc Meridon stood between her and the bright moonlight of the exit. She saw him as she had always seen him, with his somber dark eyes and the wistful smile that twisted her heart a little, even now.

"Mrs. Aronson, you are surprisingly troublesome," he said quietly.

Behind her Arthur urged, "Don't argue. Pass him."

Kay took several halting steps but Marc Meridon did not move. Suddenly Arthur lunged past her and pulled off the red scarf Marc wore. Kay stared in horror. The pale flesh of Marc's throat was a gaping wound, only just beginning to heal. He smiled, his eyebrows raised in that satiric way of his. She ran past him, stumbling blindly into the sweet, clean air, Arthur close behind.

Kay was weeping with relief when they finally stopped on the highway and looked back up the mountain, now shrouded in darkness as the moon moved overhead. After a moment she said, "Why?"

"You mean, why didn't he destroy us? I don't believe it's Meridon's way. His victims destroy themselves. . . ."

Other Pinnacle Books by Virginia Coffman:

Chalet Diabolique

VIRGINIA COFFMAN

PINNACLE BOOKS   LOS ANGELES

CHALET DIABOLIQUE

Copyright © 1971 by Virginia Coffman

A Pinnacle Books edition, published by special arrangement with the author's agent, Jay Garon-Brooke Associates.

First printing, May 1978

ISBN: 0-523-40140-X

Cover illustration by Bruce Minney

Printed in the United States of America

PINNACLE BOOKS, INC.
One Century Plaza
2029 Century Park East
Los Angeles, California 90067

Chalet Diabolique

ONE

It was the first time he had screamed during the daylight. Until now, the nightmares never troubled him when he rested in the afternoons, but only in the hours before dawn.

Kay Aronson shivered, dropped her pen and pushed the chair back from her desk. Standing still, with the stiff, nervous immobility she had developed since her husband's illness, she listened. If it was just one of Leo's nightmares, he would make no more sounds. But this time it might indicate that he was in pain. The rapid progress of his arthritic disease made any reaction possible.

She had grown used to his occasional groans or cries during a dream in the night, when those dark hours must be interminable for a man of Leo Aronson's vitality and brilliance. But on this particular afternoon the timing was unusual enough to alarm Kay, though she was perfectly aware of his sensitivity about the nightmares. He hated to have these betraying sounds noticed.

She went out into the hall and listened again.

1

Arthur Dugald, his secretary, hurried out of the library at the same time. He had been on the telephone, getting stock market closings for his employer.

"Was that Mr. Aronson?"

Kay was standing at the foot of the wide, antebellum wooden staircase, staring up at the second floor.

"A dream, I think. He has been lying down for half an hour. He gets these nightmares sometimes."

Nevertheless, and in spite of the silence from Leo Aronson's bedroom suite upstairs, she started up to him. The Virginia sunlight, bright and cheerful in spite of the January day, filtered through the uncurtained oriole window on the stair landing and comforted her a little. But she was aware of the prickling doubts, the questions about her husband's nightmares building daily, almost hourly. The nightmares had begun shortly after the mid-Atlantic accident involving one of Leo's Aronson Line jets, London bound, which dropped ten thousand feet before levelling off to a safe, if unscheduled, landing at Shannon Airport. The mishap, though harmless to everything but the nerves of the crew and Leo's fellow board members, had given Leo a whiplash injury which complicated his growing arthritic condition.

And almost immediately, the nightmares began, about whose subject he was curiously secretive, even to his wife. Perhaps he felt she wouldn't understand. She was more than twenty years younger than the attractive, fifty-five-year-old tycoon who was only just his wife's height. But even with the handicap of recent ill-health, he managed to carry himself with his back straight, his magnificent head high, and his shrewd, farseeing eyes as penetrating as ever, though still impenetrable.

Kay Aronson moved quietly through the upper hall to her husband's study. There was still no further sound. She crossed the room, then his dressing room and bath. The door into his bedroom was ajar. She started to knock, then withdrew her hand. If he really had been asleep, this would only disturb him.

The west window drapes in his bedroom were wide open as always. For a brave man he had a peculiar fetish about always having plenty of light in his room, at midnight as well as midday. She was just about to push the door open and peer into the room in a gingerly way when Leo Aronson called out in that voice which a long habit of command and a slight theatrical leaning had made both musical and terrifying.

"Don't pussyfoot around, damn you! Come marching in. I hate skulkers."

She pushed the door open, laughed at the expression on his face as he caught sight of her, and went over to the bed. Unlike that other Napoleon, he preferred a huge bed and was propped up against half a dozen pillows. His faintly greying brown hair looked dark against the white linen, and was tousled over his forehead as usual. He had a great shock of hair and it never looked combed.

"Good Lord, beautiful! I'd no idea it was you!" was his only apology.

As she bent over him he kissed the edge of her upper lip in his brisk way, so brisk, so business-

3

like, his acquaintances and rivals always expressed amazement at his popular reputation for sex appeal.

But during the five years of their marriage Kay had come to believe his enormous power and vitality came from a source greater, more uncommon than sex appeal. It was as though some god or devil had long ago bestowed upon him the gift of passionate belief in himself and he could therefore afford to shed this power over others.

Kay had twice married for sexual love and been twice burned financially. Her third marriage, a kind of merger of her fortune and Aronson's, had proved by far the happiest. Her third husband was the man to whom she could look up, not down, in spite of his moderate height.

"Hello, dear. Did you get your thoughts all untangled?" she asked casually, being careful not to imply that he needed either sympathy or assistance. "Getting his thoughts sorted out" was usually his excuse whenever pain or fatigue forced him to take to his bed.

"All in order." Turning his head from her, he moved his legs under the rumpled covers, hiding the sharp wince of pain it cost him. He patted the bed, "Come and sit down, Kay."

Even in this, his almost curt command, he exerted a certain power she found oddly comforting. As an heiress she herself had exerted all the power in her first two marriages, but with Leo Aronson her money, her background, were nothing. Rumor said he had begun as a street urchin in Malmo, Sweden. Thirty years later, he was one of the international tycoons.

What had occurred in between the urchin of

Malmo and the man of today? He had joked about it many times, but the dark abyss between the two was still there. Were his nightmares, which he always denied, a part of that darkness?

Kay seated herself on the bed and took his healthy hand. The other, the left, often was clawed and swollen with arthritis these days. "It *would* be my left," was his only complaint, for he was left-handed.

"Now then," he said briskly, his hard fingers closing over her hand, "have you anything planned for the rest of the winter?"

"What! But dear, are you up to?" She saw his scowl and amended quickly, "Are you free to take a vacation? I know you've complained about not finishing that Ethiopian merger, and so many other things. . . . Where did you have in mind? It's really been beautiful here this winter, compared to New York and Marbella and the little place above Villefranche. Even Florida has had a bad freezing spell."

"California."

"San Francisco? I'll call and have the Hillsborough place made ready for us. You—we'll enjoy the sun there."

"Not San Francisco. I've a little place, a kind of lodge—a chalet—down the coast. It's part of a Spa and Hot Springs called Lucifer Cove."

Curious that she had never heard of it before. He must have guessed her question because he added thoughtfully, "I haven't visited it for years. I believe it's been leased recently to some old woman. Schallert. Miss Something-Schallert. At any rate, it's time I returned there to settle a few little details."

"Details? You mean about your property there?"

He was avoiding her eyes. There was no question about it. Leo Aronson, who wasn't afraid of God or man, was avoiding her eyes. Now why? He who feared nothing except pity....

"The property. That and—well, we'll see. How does it sound to you, my little Kayo?"

This has been one of his peculiar endearments when he pursued her across several continents insisting that though two of her marriages had failed, he could be the lucky third. The first time he called her his little Kayo she had thought it an irony. She was, after all, his own height. But it soon became evident that Leo Aronson was nobody's inferior, no matter what his height. She liked that. She liked the respect she felt for him. It was easier to travel from respect to love, she found, than from infatuation to contempt.

"It sounds fine. But let's cut out all outside phone calls, and ticker tapes, and telegrams. Let's really get away from business. Just for a little while."

He laughed and shook her hand vigorously. "At Lucifer Cove there's no question of outside interference. The owner sees to that. It's exceedingly—" He searched for the right word. "Private. Definitely private."

"Oh, but Leo, everywhere we go, it's supposed to be private. And they always manage to reach you."

"You have my solemn promise, my dear, no one can reach us at the Cove. None but the clients of the Cove. And the Cove's owner, of course."

Something in his voice, some slight sardonic

note made her look at him quickly, but now he was smiling again and she read nothing but pleasant anticipation in his face.

Staring at him, she could hardly believe she had heard him cry out in a nightmare less than half an hour ago.

She ventured hesitantly, "Did you hear—I thought I heard someone scream a while ago."

He was bland, even innocent. "Really? Probably Dugald getting the shock of the day's market closings."

She laughed because he expected her to. But she knew he had cried out. What troubled his sleep? And why this sudden trip out to a place she had never heard of, and which, to all intents and purposes, sounded like a rest cure for the rich and jaded? Leo Aronson would never be jaded, if he lived to be a hundred. Of course, she amended with a sick little throb of realization, the doctors had all given her to understand that in his case, and with his stubborn adherence to a rugged regime, he might not have decades to live. Or even years.

Could there be any connection with this knowledge so closely guarded from him, and the cries that revealed his troubled sleep?

"Now then," he went on, obviously trying to draw her thoughts away from something he wished to avoid. "You will have several days to make your plans. Break a lot of those highly unnecessary appointments with hairdressers and masseuses and the rest while I'm out at the Cove getting things in order for you."

He must have known she would raise strong objections to that because when she opened her mouth, he touched it with one rough finger. "Quiet, woman! I want it this way."

"You hard-headed Swede!" But she kissed his cheek anyway, knowing that if she made further protests he would keep on being stubborn until he won. He always won. "All right. Go out to this Cove place. But please—Leo—please take care of yourself."

"Naturally. Don't I always?"

This gave her a strong urge both to laugh and cry at his perversity, but she let him see only the laugh.

He took her hand. "Remember, Kayo, you must promise me not to go there until I give you the word. Have I your promise?"

"If you'll promise to take care of yourself."

They shook hands. She inspected his lined face anxiously. "You aren't worried about this trip, are you, dear? I mean, you haven't any business problems or anything to bother you at that place?"

"No, my dear worrier! I know exactly what I'm going to do." At the widening of her expressive eyes, he added quickly, "And I'm going to do something—some things, that is—that I've always wanted to do. Enjoy myself."

She pretended to believe him but the tightness of his facial muscles, the peculiar, almost glassy look in his eyes, were not reassuring.

Kay was within minutes of leaving the Virginia house to join Leo at California's Lucifer Cove, when the news came. The reporters and two photographers zoomed around the circle drive just as Arthur Dugald was carrying out his

8

briefcase and a two-suiter bag. Kay had followed Leo's pennywise policy of cutting off the telephone service the night before, and the reporters in the lead car complained as they were piling out that they had tried and failed to reach Mrs. Aronson by phone.

Kay, who was on the stair landing when the group collided with Dugald in the doorway, said quickly, "Don't let them delay us, Arthur. Leo insists on waiting for us until the plane gets in. He said it will be very cold up in that little mountain field this time of the year." She was still in a mood of exhilaration after her last call from Leo just before the service was cut off the previous afternoon.

Dugald said something to a pushy young woman in the vanguard of the crowd. Kay could not hear his dry, expressionless voice, but she leaned over the stair rail. "If it's business, Arthur, just tell them to contact Leo's Richmond offices. God knows Leo needs his rest."

"It—it isn't that, Mrs. Aronson. I'm afraid something has happened. These are reporters. And people from Washington and Richmond television stations."

She didn't wait for more but hurried down the remaining stairs. Her mind told her this was just another case of an Aronson Shipping and Airlines merger or a new Aronson banking coup, or some other success Leo had hatched during these last few weeks when he was supposed to be recuperating. But there was the other feeling, the peculiar, prickling sensation that this was different. An oddly sinister silence gripped everyone suddenly and they were all looking at her, crowding into the elegant old colonial hall, too spacious for a chic, modern "foyer."

Kay hadn't quite reached Dugald when the foremost of the group, a young woman, pushed past the secretary and made a tentative grab at her.

"Mrs. Aronson, may we have your reaction to your husband's business ventures, as a result of the plane crash? Was Mr. Aronson on a business trip?"

Kay reached for something. It was Arthur Dugald's arm, the muscles surprisingly hard and strong. She looked at him.

"Is it true? Was there a crash? How bad?"

"His own plane. This morning. Apparently it went down over the ocean about ten minutes after it took off from the little airstrip in the Pacific Coast Range. The one—"

"The one where you and I were to land."

He nodded.

She was unaware of a surprising numbness. Everything registered. She missed nothing of the nuances, the movements and murmurs around her. But she felt nothing. She did not cry. She said calmly, hearing her voice just a half-tone higher than normal, "He couldn't have been flying away from that place. We talked yesterday. He was waiting for me. He said so. He even said he would walk up the mountain and meet us at that field."

Rather sharper than was his habit, Dugald replied to that. "Probably making a quick trip to San Francisco. Or something called him to L.A."

"No. He wouldn't. He said he would wait." She raised her head. Rising anger, fury, suspicion.

She used them all to bury the first aching sense of loss. "What happened out there? Why was he suddenly in such a hurry to leave? What is this *Lucifer Cove?*"

TWO

"We should have held the memorial service here, on top of the mountain," Kay murmured, breathing deeply the piercing air of a bright January morning.

Arthur Dugald agreed. "No California smog up here. This field must have been exactly where Mr. Aronson intended to wait for our plane." He glanced over at the mud and grass beginnings of a trail down into the valley on the far side of the mountain. "I believe we will find Lucifer Cove at the foot of that path. Hardly a freeway."

"Hardly! But if Leo, with his arthritis and bad heart, thought he could make it up that steep trail to this place, then I can certainly make it down." She started forward, determined to show the noncommittal secretary that she had always been athletically inclined. He might be pardoned for doubting this; since her Givenchy wardrobe, even in mourning, could not help being sleek, exquisitely simple, and immaculate. Nothing like it had ever been seen on this shale-strewn mountain path. Fortunately, her shoes, in their modern shape and cut, had heels suitable for walking. She looked back once, to wave goodbye to the pilot of the Aronson plane that landed her and Dugald in the meadow, but it had already taken off, with surprisingly little noise.

"I wish I could come into that Cove without letting them know me as Leo's widow," she said, more to herself than her companion.

During the tense two weeks since Leo's plane went down off the California coast with none of the bodies recovered, Kay very often felt that the secretary knew more than he claimed to know about that oddly secretive Lucifer Cove which, she was convinced, had cost Leo Aronson his life. If this were so, then the only way to discover his degree of responsibility in Leo's death was to bring him along to the Cove on what she referred to publicly as her effort to "recover in seclusion and find herself."

"I'll find more than myself!" she promised Leo's memory. "And I'll make them pay, whoever they are behind his murder." But she didn't say it aloud, nor indicate her suspicions to Arthur Dugald. She suspected the "murder" was instigated for business reasons. Some corporate enemy had chosen this complex series of moves, including his visit to Lucifer Cove, in order to destroy him. But they hadn't reckoned with his widow, that "poor little rich clothesmare, as *Women's Wear Daily* labeled her in a less inspired moment.

Dugald was studying the valley below them with a frown, but evidently he had been considering her remark in connection with the Cove. "I imagine you are too well known to deceive them.

There are many people of your social class here. They will have seen you in *Bazaar* and *Vogue* and *Town and Country*." The lighter quality in his voice, its hint of irony and contempt, was not lost on her.

Good! she thought. . . . Let him despise me. If he really was in this conspiracy, the less he respects me, the less suspicious he will be.

He had been surprised when she did not bring her maid with her on her visit to the Cove, and she was briefly afraid he would be suspicious of that. But she couldn't afford to have the eagle-eyed woman around her constantly while she was trying to give an impression of herself as shallow, giddy, and not exactly grief-stricken to find herself one of the richest widows in the world. She let Dugald believe she was swayed by his assurance that there would be plenty of competent maid service at the Cove.

At the same time, she very much wanted Arthur Dugald nearby, to watch him, though her excuse was that he must wind up any business affairs involving her late husband at the Cove.

"How on earth do people find this place?" she asked, staring down at the mountain-locked little valley that trailed northward far below her feet. "They certainly don't all land private planes up in that meadow and hike down this poor excuse for a path."

"Most clients drive in," the secretary explained. "The entrance is exceedingly difficult to find."

"It must be." She put one gloved hand to the rim of her big sunglasses and shaded her eyes as she walked down the trail, surveying the place she was convinced had somehow enticed Leo to his death.

Just beyond the foot of the trail the single north-south street bisecting the valley connected an expensive-looking Spa with the sprawling Hot Springs at the north end of the valley. Sulphur issued forth from the clump of buildings as if the whole Hot Springs were going up in smoke, an acrid, yellow series of fumes hellish to see and to smell.

There seemed to be no village thoroughfares beyond that single main street running past the Spa to the Hot Springs, but to the West of the Spa and all the way to the low coastal series of hills there was a tangled cloverleaf of roads slicing through arid ground that was occasionally perforated by spirals of ugly sulphur fumes. If those roads did lead to the Pacific Coast Highway and the ocean, the exit and the great highway itself was hidden from Kay's view by an especially ominous granite pile and by the low range which formed the western boundary of the little valley.

"Sentinel Rock, I believe they call it," said Dugald, behind her, pointing to the granite pile. "It hides the only official entrance to the Cove." Dugald never did anything overt that could be held against him, or reported, but in his quiet, unobstrusive personality there was a persistence and a constant talent for predicting her moves, even her thoughts. He probably wanted to assure himself of his position after Leo's death, but that hardly seemed reason enough to put up with his persistent first-guessing which got on her nerves.

Kay looked down the winding, shale and dust path below her feet. She said with irony, "If Sentinel Rock is the only official entrance, what do they call this spacious autobahn? How on earth did Leo make it down this trail?" It made her sick to think of the way Leo must have plunged ahead down the path with only his pilot, a very insecure reed, to lean on, and with his left knee giving him fits with its arthritic knot.

"I assure you, Mrs. Aronson, the Cove is a very exclusive Spa. In fact, it's remarkably difficult even to find the entrance over there on the coast highway."

All that might be true, Kay thought, but it didn't explain why Leo, with his painful complications, had not only insisted on visiting an inaccessible place in an area not noted for its cures, but had actually preferred to come in by this secretive way, rather than the obvious entrance. Although it had everything, she knew he had disliked his Rolls because it suggested creaking age and foreign royalty. His latest Italian sports car was beyond him the moment he left for the Cove, but the American cars would have provided some comfort without calling too much attention to him as one of the world's billionaires.

Apparently, Arthur Dugald was still hooked on the idea that Kay Forrest Aronson disapproved of the Cove because it wasn't exclusive enough. He began again about the "special qualities" of this mysterious little Spa whose extraordinary value for Leo baffled his wife.

She cut in as politely as she could. Because she disliked him, she tried a little too hard to be civil. "What on earth was his attachment to this place?"

Dugald said, "As we walk down the path, you

16

will see his chalet on that trail ledge to your left, west of us and halfway down. That was Mr. Aronson's retreat. It was a remarkable view of the entire valley."

On the ledge trail which seemed to branch out from the path they had taken, Kay saw a small, exquisite white building made in the style of a classic Greek temple. They would have to pass it to reach Leo's chalet, a bright, cozy-looking wood building at the far side of the trail.

"What is that pretty white building? Looks as though it might be made of stone."

"The pilot told me it is being used currently as a devil's temple. A young lady, Nadine Janos, at the Cove, conducts services every few nights. They call her the Devil's Priestess."

Kay studied the building, murmuring, "What a shame! It might have been on the Acropolis, it's so lovely. Couldn't it be used for a museum or something?"

"I believe it is more profitably employed in its present use," said the secretary, dryly.

So Leo's nearest neighbor, in this queer little valley so effectively cut off from the world, had been a coven of devil worshippers! This matter alone seemed too absurd to be taken seriously; yet there was an ugliness about it, a kind of creeping evil. She was not religious but here, under the blue sky of this brisk January morning, she couldn't help feeling that she would prefer a house of normal worship nearby, and the mystery of Leo's trip, his nightmares, his death, gave a special and sinister importance to the temple.

Devil worship! What was Leo thinking of to move into a house next to such idiocy and even

17

downright evil? It was unlikely that this devil's priestess woman would be answering prayers for the good of humanity. Did the woman have anything to do with Leo's death; or rather, his flight from here that resulted in his death?

Kay squared her shoulders and walked down the steep path, reminding herself that she had come here to find out this very thing. Something had drawn Leo to Lucifer Cove. She was going to find out what that was, and see to it that—some way—the guilty were punished! It was little enough to do for Leo Aronson, who had done so much for her.

Kay hefted the neat little crimson Hartmann bag which contained her makeup and a few items of jewelry, and she increased her pace. She knew she was deliberately trying to escape Arthur Dugald, and it was childish, because, of course, there was no escaping the ubiquitous secretary. He was one of her prime suspects. He knew too much about all this.

He didn't help matters by beginning on the touchy matter of her husband's nightmares.

"Pardon, Mrs. Aronson, but I'm wondering if you have learned anything helpful about Mr. Aronson's dreams."

She laughed tersely. "I might have, if there had been a little more . . . time." Her voice broke slightly but she recovered at once. She glanced at him, wondering, as always, what he already knew. He was not a man for the ladies. She couldn't remember a time when he had spent his free time on women. On the other hand, he was never very far from Kay in what seemed to be an attempt to make himself as indispensable to her as he was to her husband. There was certainly no effort at romancing her.

"By the way," she went on, watching him. "Who—precisely—is or are the management of this place?"

But she wasn't sure he had heard her. Arthur Dugald was gesturing to the village that trickled northward, bisecting the valley with its single main street that began slightly to the north of the muddy ditch and a simple plank bridge at the foot of the path which they were descending. The bridge was probably no more than half a mile from their present spot but the path took so many twists and turns and was so steep it seemed further.

"There. I think you will enjoy the Spa. It has almost everything for everyone, I'm told. Pools, a superb dining salon and cuisine, and several remarkably varied and attractive bars. Gaming. The usual Sauna. Very like the Roman Baths, with something for everyone. Further up the street there, the shop with the Regency front, has everything. Any possible request you'll find Mrs. Peasecod can fill. She looks a bit of an old witch, but she has connections. Any products. Drugs ... anything."

She wondered what that sly little hint was supposed to indicate. She had never been attracted to the drug scene. Was he hoping she would be, or merely warning her?

"So we are perched up here above the world," she remarked, avoiding his hint. "I should think Leo would have preferred the Spa, if it has so much to make life easier. But of course," she added, guessing the secretary's next reminder, "my husband preferred not to have things made easy." Dugald's faint smile made her say quickly, "That was one of his greatest fascinations as a man. If there was a challenge, he took it up every time." *And so will I*, she thought . . . *So will I, my friend.*

"We turn here."

She saw the ledge trail which branched off behind a prickly cypress that had been twisted and scarred by years of salt wind and coastal fog. Once on the trail she noticed how the Janos woman's temple with its neat portico and doric pillars loomed up in the crisp golden light, blotting out everything else, the mountainside behind it, and the two-story chalet further along the ledge trail, with its blue and yellow and red wooden "alpine" decorations and its rounded front with innumerable windows.

Kay tried to ignore the Greek Temple. No one was around it. The place was apparently deserted except for a little striped gray tabby cat who sat among the doric pillars, calmly licking his paw while he watched Kay and Dugald pass by. Kay laughed uneasily.

"I get the feeling I'm being dissected by his eyes."

Dugald did not look back. "Oh, that. It's only Kinkajou. Kind of the official Cove cat, they tell me. You'll see him everywhere. If you don't like cats, I would advise you not to let him know. Like most felines, he'll hang around you constantly. They are perverse creatures."

"Yes. I know cats. And I know their sense of humor. I like them. Or rather . . ." She glanced over her shoulder, and, in spite of Dugald's attempt to make it all very sinister, she could not help smiling. "I admire them, their incomparable grace, their independence. Kinkajou really looks quite harmless."

Dugald's frown and shrug annoyed her but she pretended not to notice, since he clearly intended that she should be influenced.

"You know Lucifer Cove like a native," she remarked pleasantly. "Or do you absorb it through your pores?"

He showed excellent teeth in a smile. "I listen."

She didn't doubt that for a minute. She stepped up on the porch, holding out her hand, palm up. "The key the Cove sent you, Arthur?"

"Of course." He dropped it into her palm. She hadn't quite touched the lock when the door opened abruptly, startling her in spite of herself.

A thin pillar of black and white stood there in the doorway, staring at her. Kay was amused to see that the pillar, female variety, looking taller than it actually was, had been caught by surprise. The pillar was actually a young woman, under thirty, wearing a long-sleeved, ankle-length white gown sprinkled with cabalistic signs. Her lengthy, straight black hair looked unreal in the sunlight. A wig, obviously. But it was her eyes that Kay suspected could be hypnotic. Ever so slightly prominent, they were a large and smoky blue. The rest of the face was nothing. The young woman needed nothing but those extraordinary eyes. And her voice. Clearly, it was a voice schooled to sway multitudes.

Like worshippers of the devil?

"Good morning, Mrs. Aronson. May I offer my condolences? I knew your husband . . ." As Kay's eyebrows went up, the young woman added, ". . . slightly. He found our temple services interesting. I am Nadine Janos, priestess to My Lord Satan."

Kay smiled. "Yes. I imagined you must be." She was moving around the priestess, reaching for the door. She had made no reference to Nadine's presence here, but the Janos woman was not completely obtuse.

"I have been collecting some of the literature I left with L—Mr. Aronson. About the temple." She held up her left arm. Among the folds of the big, dramatic sleeve were several pamphlets. On the cover of the top one Kay read what she considered the crux of the whole Satan bit: SATAN REPAYS IN KIND—GIFT OFFERINGS THAT HAVE REACHED MY LORD SATAN.

How Leo must have laughed at the obviousness of that!

When neither Kay nor Dugald said anything the priestess tucked away her pamphlets, stepped away from the door, and started along the path. She looked back. "Mrs. Aronson, just for laughs, you might drop in at the temple while you are here . . . and discover what interested your late husband so much."

Kay did not go into the house for a full minute or two as she watched the woman's sinuous black and white form moving away. Then, remembering her companion, and curious over his reaction, she glanced his way. But as usual, his fact was

22

impassive. It was awkward to discover that his gaze had been fixed on Kay herself.

Was he curious over her interest in the devil's priestess? Or was he studying her own reactions for some reason?

THREE

It was an astonishing interior for what appeared to be a standard chalet of the kind seen so frequently in Austria and Switzerland. They entered the main room abruptly. The living room was round, with a huge fireplace at the far side, depressingly black and dead in a place already darkened by the closed shutters. Beside the fireplace was a door, partially opened to the kitchen. In the center of the room, however, Kay found to her great surprise, a spiral flight of metal steps winding upward through a hole in the ceiling to what must clearly be the sleeping quarters. The neat, round hole in the ceiling was outlined by a metal railing, she was relieved to see.

"I hope nobody ever walks in his sleep in this place," she remarked.

Dugald was looking upward too. "No," he agreed. "That would be a trifle—dangerous." He glanced around the big room in which they stood. "There don't seem to be any bedrooms downstairs."

He said this with no inflection whatever, which

amused Kay very much. She wondered if it would be possible to disconcert him in any way. In short, was he human? To test him she laughed and suggested lightly, "It would shock the natives, I suppose, if both our bedrooms were on the same floor."

He actually reddened a little and his cool blue eyes blinked, making him not unattractive; they showed him to be vulnerable. Kay had reached some slight drop of humanity in him. He tried to cover this by suggesting, "Naturally, I will be putting up in the village in these circumstances. But you will need a maid here, or a companion. If you wish, I can arrange that."

She started up the metal steps. "Yes. You might do that." She looked down over the metal rail. "No signs of Leo at all . . . nothing left the way he would leave it. It's as if he had never lived here."

Without glancing around, Dugald explained, "I understand a woman named Schallert had leased the place, and when Mr. Aronson decided to visit here she was moved elsewhere. There is a good deal more elegance in the Spa. I sppose that is where she is staying now."

She had taken several more steps, a trifle annoyed by her nervous reaction to the metallic click of her own footsteps, when the secretary called up to her from the living room.

"It was my impression that Mr. Aronson was not fond of television, excepting his own commercials. Am I wrong?"

She was now so high above him she had to bend her knees to see him far below in the murky dusk of the shuttered room.

25

"You are never wrong, Arthur." That sounded even ruder and more sardonic than she had meant it to, and she tried to soften it with the added reminder, "Which is why my husband found you indispensable. What is it about television? What makes you ask?"

"Nothing." But he had left the foot of the steps and crossed the room below, out of her sight. Shortly afterward there were sounds of furniture being shoved, and a squawk as if dozens of rusty hinges were forced at once.

She reached the top of the steps, took hold of the rail which protected the person or persons sleeping in that curious bed-sitting room, and for some reason found herself more interested in the behavior of Arthur Dugald than in examining the room in which her husband had slept, and where she expected to sleep.

"What it is, Arthur? What did you find? More cats? Or another of those sexy devil worshippers?"

His laugh, short and light, but undeniably a laugh, came to her as another surprise about him. He really was getting almost human. His voice began a little muffled as he spoke from somewhere in the shadowy regions of the room below, then became more natural as he approached the steps and looked up at her.

"Someone forgot to turn off the television sets. The place seems to be more than amply supplied. One in the living room. One in the kitchen, and—if I'm not mistaken—one at the bottom of the cellar steps."

"This place has a cellar?"

He started up the steps, his face growing more

human as it ascended above the shuttered lower regions. Fortunately, the shutters were not closed in the bed-sitting room where Kay now stood. The resulting light from a wind-swept blue sky made the room look cozy and even warm, thanks to the preponderance of flame-colored blankets, rugs and throw pillows.

"I don't believe the cellar is used much. The door is under the biggest television set. One of those root cellars you don't see on the Pacific Coast, I expect. I doubt if Mr. Aronson even knew it was there. Although . . ." He frowned.

Uneasy without quite knowing why, she prompted him. "Although what?"

"The dust is so thick on the steps you can see footprints clearly. A woman. With small feet."

"Probably the Schallert woman who used to leave the house. Good heavens! What a delightful room!" She began to walk around the room, which was semi-circular, with a curve of innumerable front windows facing north. There was a marvelous view of the entire little valley of Lucifer Cove. "And window seats. How wonderful! I haven't seen any for years. . . ." But the secretary's mind was obviously not on window seats. "Is there something else?" she asked, seeing that he still stared at the spiral steps and by implication the things he had seen on the ground floor.

He started slightly. "Not anything that I can be sure of. But the cellar must be larger than I thought."

"Why? It can't be too large. We are perched on the side of a mountain, after all."

"Nevertheless, she must have come back up somehow."

He must be deliberately trying some scare technique. Pretending she had not found his uneasiness the least contagious, she said with an unexpected harsh, excited note in her voice. "Didn't she?"

"There is only one set of prints. Down. The electricity is on. I studied the prints. I don't think I was mistaken."

"Well," she dismissed this with a conviction she no longer felt. "She certainly wouldn't find it comfortable to stay down there; so there must be another way up."

He said calmly, "It may connect with the temple. There can't be more than a quarter of a mile between them. I wonder if . . ." He went to one of the windows and looked out, then back at Kay. She finished his thought.

"You wonder if that is how Nadine Janos got into this house this morning."

He nodded. She went to the window and stood beside him, staring out.

"No. You said your precious footprints went down, not up."

He smiled faintly. "From the way she moved along, one wonders if she touched the ground at all."

This made her laugh and she wondered briefly if she had misjudged her husband's secretive and protective secretary all this time. At least, he sounded sincere, about that self-styled devil's priestess.

"There is bound to be a logical explanation of your ghostly footsteps," she told him, wondering if she dared to pursue the dark question of Leo's death with him. Not that she trusted him any more than ever. But they were at least making conversation, which was a step ahead of their old relationship.

"Arthur, in spite of that silly report of probable engine failure, have you ever wondered about my husband's death?"

He turned away from the fabulous view out the windows. "No," he said, without a single inflection that she could catch, but then, the single syllable answer did not leave much room for improvisation.

"You haven't wondered? I mean . . ." She didn't know what she meant precisely. If she went any further, she would reveal her own suspicions, and she had little doubt that if he and/or someone in Lucifer Cove got the idea she was searching for Leo's murderers, she would soon find herself in one of those accidental aircraft disasters. Or even something handier, like a fall down that cliff beyond the path. She bit off further questions and then, just as she had given up, the secretary cleared his throat. The small sound startled her after the troubling little silence that preceded it.

"I meant to say, I haven't wondered about Mr. Aronson's death so much as I have wondered about his nightmares."

She stared at him. "Of course. But they go together; don't they?"

"On the contrary. They do not go together. The nightmares came *before* the plane crash."

He was right, but the puzzling thing had been his calling her attention to the fact. Especially if he himself was part of the murder plan, or even

29

knew about it, as she suspected. She shrugged off his suggestion.

"I suppose so, but I can't see the difference myself. I rather like this room. Maybe I'll like it downstairs as well when we have the shutters opened. What else is up here?"

He walked across the room. Beyond the curved stair rail was a door, the only door in the room. They looked in together. It was a large, old-fashioned but well-fitted bathroom, with a comfortable, deep bathtub. "That would be Leo's doing," she pointed out. The shower was a more European attachment. "He hated showers," she explained. Then she added quickly, "But you know his habits as well as I do."

He didn't bother to deny it.

There was another door out of the bathroom on the far side. When Dugald tried the door, it was locked.

"That's odd," Kay murmured. But the efficient Dugald tried various keys from the envelope in the pocket of his topcoat. When one of them worked, he pushed the door open into darkness. Kay snapped on the bathroom overhead light and from this, they were able to make out the furnishings in the darkened, shuttered room.

"Another bedroom, and there appears to be only one bath on this floor," Kay said without enthusiasm. "This room is furnished; isn't it? But not pleasant, I think. Not charming like the other one."

"It was used by two of the ah . . . friends of the previous tenant."

"Miss Schallert's friends? But it looks like. Well, not a woman's room at all." He smiled and she understood belatedly. "Somehow, I didn't think the Schallert woman would be having boyfriends here. Have they all moved down to the Spa?"

Arthur Dugald said in his quiet way, "Only Miss Schallert intended to move down, I believe."

"And her gentlemen?"

"She knew them singly. One of them died at the Cove last Spring. A man named Standish, I'm told. And then, quite recently, an oil man. Hemplemeier."

She shivered. "Whether they died here or down at the Spa, this room looks so depressing. I can almost feel the presence of the poor devils." She backed into the bathroom. "Lock the door again, please."

When they were in the bright, cheerful bed-sitting room, she tried to throw off the depression of that discovery. "I'll say one thing for this place. For a health spa it has a pretty unhealthy record."

"Yes. I suspect there is a great deal more to the Cove than just a health spa."

She looked at him but the old, familiar blankness had closed over his features. She couldn't tell what he was thinking.

"Well," she lied briskly, with a shrug, "it's not my concern. I came here to . . ." She broke off. She could hardly add in this determined voice that she was here merely to recover from Leo's death.

The obstinate Dugald took this opportunity to show an interest in her. "Yes, Mrs. Aronson?"

She gave him a look she hoped was as bland and unreadable as his own. "I think it should be obvious. It's a kind of tribute to my husband. I want to feel the peace—or whatever it was he found during that last day of his life, before he decided to take his plane out of here."

He surprised her by asking suddenly, "Don't you think it might be interesting to know *why* Mr. Aronson decided to take the plane out of this valley?"

She found herself evading his eyes. "That too, of course. But I think the investigation pretty well settled that. He must have intended to fly to San Francisco for that conference on cargoliners, those awful container ships."

A peculiar "ting-ting" sound somewhere in the house startled them both. In ordinary circumstances either Kay or the ever-alert Dugald would have recognized the obvious ring of a telephone, but it took both of them more than five minutes to find the phone, hidden as it was in a drawer of an anachronistic highboy.

"What on earth? . . ." Kay took the neat little phone that the secretary handed to her, and whispered stupidly, "Why do you suppose he hid the phone?"

"Tired of hearing it ring?"

She smiled, but it was the most likely answer. The voice came through, all feminine cheer, faceless and false at the other end of that dainty pink earpiece.

"Welcome to Lucifer Cove, Mrs. Aronson. How did you find your cottage?"

"Very presentable, thank you. Who is this, please?"

"I'm Bonnie Lou Bryer, Ma'am. Down at the Spa. I'm on the reception desk as you enter. I'm kind of thrilled. Like you, Ma'am, it's my first day here at the Spa. I worked my way up from the Hot Springs." The girl went rambling on, then broke into giggles about "working her way up" which Kay could only guess at.

Arthur Dugald was trying to look less interested than he obviously felt, and had gone over to examine the furniture against the far walls of the room, but he looked back as Kay was trying to revive the girl on the phone.

"Yes, Miss Bryer?" She looked over the telephone at him. "Miss Bonnie Lou Bryer."

He laughed. "I don't believe it." But she saw that he was doing something to a large portable television set.

While the girl on the phone was inviting Kay down to the Spa and asking when she would like a maid sent up, her mind was on the curious actions of the secretary.

"I'll be down to the Spa shortly and discuss this with the management." Kay wanted to meet the people who ran this valley enterprise as soon as possible. If they weren't involved in what had happened to Leo, they might, at least, betray some clue that would lead to a Cove client who had a motive or some connection with her husband. She had some names burned on her brain, names of business enemies, business rivals, tycoons who wanted to amalgamate many of his holdings. Somewhere at Lucifer Cove she was convinced there had to be a name, a connection.

"We'll have the red carpet out, Mrs. Aronson," the bubbly, too-happy voice promised. "You don't mind hiking down the trail? We have a lift, a sort of ski lift that's going in just east of the trail, but it isn't quite completed yet."

"Perfectly all right. I like to walk."

There were more amenities, more good wishes, then a little click. Kay was putting the phone back but held it a moment as she watched Dugald across the room. But another and unexpected sound, caught her in the gesture of setting the phone back on its cradle. It was a second click.

She frowned, completed her gesture and then asked with some amusement, "Will you please tell me what you are doing over there?"

He hesitated. He was studying the set. "I was turning off your television set."

"What!"

At the extraordinary nervousness in that single syllable, he came toward her. "Probably Mr. Aronson left in a hurry." She looked at him. He went on quickly. "In a hurry for the San Francisco meeting."

"And left the television on! Arthur, he's been gone over two weeks. And the place has been cleaned, put in order. You'd think somebody would turn off a few sets."

"There is a perfectly normal explanation, you know."

She found herself shuddering and when he stared at her, she agreed, with a small, hollow laugh, making meaningless motions of tucking back strands of pale, blonde hair as if the gestures were somehow signs of extreme calm.

"Naturally. Everything has been perfectly normal. I'm beginning to think Leo was simply frightened into running away. What a grisly place this is! What with TVs on for weeks, and footsteps in cellars and . . ."

"That was merely an observation. I'm not foolproof. Maybe the lady came up the steps backward."

"And that ghastly second bedroom! I can almost feel the presence of those two dead men. Whether they died there or not, I'm sure there's some—some unhappiness connected with the room." She reached the stair rail. "Now, I'm going down to that elegant Spa you talked about, and try and relax for an hour or two."

He followed her after a moment. "Shall I have your things unpacked and put away?"

"Thank you. I'd be grateful for anything you do about this place. I just want to be with human beings for a while."

"Thank you."

The irony was lost on her. She felt badly shaken and bone tired. Maybe it was the long delayed reaction to Leo's death. She hurried down the spiral steps, making a terrific clatter on the metal, but not caring very much. In the dusk of the big living room she passed the door into the kitchen, then remembered the cellar door in the floor. Cellars were more or less out of her sphere, but Dugald's remarks had aroused her curiosity. She went around the steps to the large and clumsy television console. Arthur Dugald had moved it along the floor, as he told her, exposing the cellar door in the floor. But he had not returned the console to its former position.

Or had he? It was perfectly true that there were drag marks on the polished hardwood floor showing were the console had been moved, revealing the cellar door, but it seemed to Kay that even in the dusky atmosphere, there were fade marks on the edge of the carpet near where the console was set now.

Above her, the secretary started down the steps. Before Kay could remember her suspicions of his conduct, she looked up.

"You moved this television set?"

"Yes. I imagine you can see the marks. But it is simple enough to move back. I merely thought you would prefer to know the cellar existed." He moved faster, clearly puzzled by her sudden, intense concern over such a small matter as the moving of a piece of furniture.

"No. It's not that. Arthur . . . look. The console used to be almost exactly where you moved it. So it looks as if I—or maybe Leo—was not supposed to know about the cellar. Doesn't that strike you as a little weird?"

He said nothing but hurried down, swung around the stair rail and looked the situation over. Then he went over to the north windows, drew the drapes open. Somewhat more light seeped in through the shutters but it only revealed what Kay had already discovered.

She looked at him, sorry now that she had blurted out her suspicions. His eyes had that ageless, unreadable blue light she often saw in very deep ocean waters. She backed away a step. He pretended not to notice but bent to examine the old indentations on the edge of the carpet. When he stood she was several feet away, and he seemed so noncommittal, so very much the secretary she wondered how she could have had that sudden fear of him, or of his keen intelligence. She returned to him and he released the hook on the cellar door, opening it. There was an electric light, small and shaded, on one side of the wall going down. Dugald pressed the switch. Together, he and Kay saw the stairs, dusty but with small heel marks, small, out-of-fashion pointed toes where the sole had come down on the dust. At the foot of the wooden stairs in the narrow passage that seemed to lead north and down further under the mountain, someone had left a television set on its wheeled stand. The set was undoubtedly broken. It seemed some years out of date, and they assumed it had simply been discarded.

Kay said, "What should we do about it?"

"Do you want to examine the place? I know there are tunnels and caves over the coast range, around Hollister in central California. A place they call the Pinnacles has wandering passages like this."

"No. No. Let's not go down there now. Maybe, with more people, later—but not now."

He nodded. They stood up. He hooked the cellar door closed. "You won't want it opened at night, particularly."

"Heavens, no! Thank you. I'll report it down at the Spa and have them investigate." She turned and started out of the house. She thought he was going to leave it at that, the obedient secretary. But as she was going down the front steps, he appeared, surprisingly fast, in the doorway.

"Mrs. Aronson."

"Yes?"

"May I make a suggestion?"

She did not have to agree. She stopped and waited.

"Don't speak of this at the Spa. To anyone." She started to ask why when he cut in quickly, "Not until we learn more about the Cove, and what made Mr. Aronson fly out so suddenly that last morning."

She moistened her dry lips, aware that her whole trim body was stiff with tension.

"All right. I won't say anything. Not now, anyway."

FOUR

At midday the little sheltered world of Lucifer Cove looked singularly innocent to Kay Aronson as she strolled down the trail to the valley below. As she passed the prickly mesquite, the ancient, twisted cypress trees, and the new green shoots of nameless weeds, she felt infinitely better. She began to wonder how she could ever had let herself become frightened over absurdities like cellars and a bedroom slept in by two men at widely separated times, who had both died elsewhere.

"It's not like me," she thought. "I'm like Leo. I make up my mind. I do things or don't do them. I know what I suspect and I follow up." But now, she wasn't sure what she suspected or how she would follow up. After a five year acquaintance with the inhuman perfection of her husband's trusted secretary, Arthur Dugald, she had quite suddenly—and disconcertingly—begun to suspect he was human. Whether he was evilly human or innocently human she hadn't the least idea. At the moment she leaned toward the idea that he might possibly be innocent. It would make life in the immediate future a little brighter to know there was someone she could trust. As Leo had trusted him? Funny. She had forgotten that. Leo was usually such a good judge of character.

Little sounds aroused her to the clear, salt-tanged air around her. The angry, insulted spitting of a cat, and a growling noise, as if a dog were vigorously worrying something. Definitely a large dog. Dogs were a knowledgeable matter to her, as were cats. "One of the few talents I was reared with," she thought cynically. But there had always been dogs, large and small, on the Forrest Estates, both as guards and as pets. There had been cats too, intriguing in their mystery, their beauty, and grace and independence. And somewhere along the heavily wooded slope she was witness to what was obviously a cat and dog fight.

She stopped, looked around beyond the stony path, into thickets that bordered both sides of the path. On her left, almost directly beneath Miss Janos' white temple, which cast a narrow noon-day shadow over the scene, Kay noted the violent thrashing in the underbrush.

Kay picked up a twisted branch among the debris on the side of the trail and taking steps as long as her A-line skirt permitted, managed to get into the center of the underbrush, just inches away from the carnage. Briefly, she reflected that she had just shot a pair of hose but it was in a good cause.

A huge, liver-colored hound had caught Kinkajou, the little gray-striped tabby cat, by the throat and was shaking it viciously amid a cacophony of growls. The cat was now mute and in a

40

bad way. Its great, glowing eyes were nearly closed. There was blood clotting its striped coat.

Kay gasped and raised the twisted branch. The little cat was pitiful, but it was also oddly appealing. Kay felt a surge of fury flow over the length of her arm as she struck the hound across the haunches. It took several hard blows, whose effect was less due to pain than the surprise inflicted, but the hound leaped ahead to escape this attack from the rear, crashed into a prickly mesquite bush, backed off and looked at her. In that second she could have sworn he grinned at her, his teeth all gleaming. As she started to go after him, the creature leaped forward, plunging along the mountainside between the bushes.

The hound outran her in no time, and when his lean body with its pale-liver color had been camouflaged among the dry growths of the mountain, Kay made her way back to the spot where the one-sided combat had taken place. Her exquisitely cut dress and sleeveless jerkin were a mass of stains, pulled threads and slashes from their contact with innumerable twigs, and her pale blonde hair had pulled loose from its fashionable coiffure, tendrils trailing down in front of her eyes.

"I'm certainly a mess, and it's all your fault. Poor little puss," she said playfully as she came back to the tiny clearing where she had left the injured Kinkajou. The gouts of blood were there in the dust, a little trail of them. And then, abruptly, nothing.

Where had the poor thing dragged itself to die? She looked around, parted the bushes, searched in every direction, but it soon became evident that the cat had crawled surprisingly far to die. She came back to the bloody spots, already drying to a dingy, faded brown, and, to her horror, found herself crying. Her eyes burned, her throat felt choked. She reacted much more violently than she had when she first heard of the plane crash.

She felt in the pocket of her jerkin for a handkerchief, usually used for decorative purposes. "What's the matter with me? I don't even know the little cat. Thousands of cats die every day." But it was just as if she had suddenly lost dear, comfortable, stubborn Leo all over again.

"Here, Kinkajou . . . Come here . . . Come here little cat . . ." She made friendly noises but nothing happened. Then she dabbed her eyes, relieved that she wore a minimum of mascara and no false lashes, and made her way back to the trail, still hoping she might catch sight of the little cat and bring him down to whatever surgical talent Lucifer Cove possessed. They might think she was crazy, but there was an aura of money usually evoked by her name, and whatever people thought of her, they seldom told her so.

She saw nothing like Kinkajou on the way down, although there were occasional noises in the bushes, probably birds and jack rabbits she thought. A cypress tree grew at the side of the trail, its sharp, dry branches like arthritic fingers, beckoning across the trail. The path looped around it and under an overhanging ledge of the mountainside. Kay made her way around the tree and into the path that headed almost precipitously down to the plank bridge over a dry gulch on the floor of the valley.

Voices should have warned her, but she was

wrapped in her confused, tormented thoughts, including persistent images of the injured little cat, and it came as a distinct shock when she nearly walked into a stout woman in tight pantsuit and fringed poncho, and a thinnish woman, perhaps older, who looked exceedingly nervous and seemed to be saying something she had repeated often before.

"But I do feel so . . . so self-conscious when I think about going up to the Hot Springs and—you know—signing in. All that makeup and the clothes! What would the young man think of me? After all, he works in the Mirror Room Bar at the Spa, hearing all the gossip of the Cove. He's sure to know how old . . ."

"Not at all, Marge. Believe me, it's common as dirt here. We all . . . they all do it."

"Do what?" asked the thin woman, echoing Kay's sudden curiosity.

"Get their way, I mean. It's part of being at the Cove. What else do we pay for? Or sign for? You wait 'til you see Miss Janos' temple up here. Maybe we can get inside and look around. The charisma is marvelous. The pentagram—the very sight of what it symbolizes—is too marvelous."

They had paid almost no attention to Kay as they passed her beyond a brief, unfriendly glance from the fat one. This Lucifer Cove was beginning to sound like the answer to a number of sexual prayers of these women, and even less like a covey of plotters who would manipulate a plane crash at sea for no practical purpose that Kay could see at the moment. In fact, her whole wild suspicion just possibly could prove ludicrous.

Then what? It seemed to her now that if she

43

couldn't avenge Leo, if his death had really been accidental—stupid and without purpose—the rest of her life would be the same. Maybe it would be different later. She only knew how she felt at this minute in time. Her lover and friend, confidant and companion, the man who had been both husband and father, was gone. She didn't want to have time to think of the loss, the lonely time ahead. Better to keep busy. Better to apply her thoughts to the puzzle of things like Arthur Dugald's real nature, or that odd and rather unpleasant cellar passage. Or even the management of Lucifer Cove which, in its spare time, must act as a Lonely Hearts Bureau.

A cool, invigorating salt wind blew in from the coast along the dry gulley which was lined with rocks, dead leaves, twigs and branches, the debris of flash floods. Several people were on the rough plank bridge, the young, athletic ones hiking up the trail she had left. But there were a number of men and women obviously in their fifties and sixties, the males wearing aloha shirts, the women in dated mini skirts, both sexes bedecked with fringe. She smiled, privately wishing them well.

The trail ended at the bridge. By the time she had crossed the gulley, she found herself on the main street of Lucifer Cove. At the far north end was the great sulphur-shrouded hulk of the Hot Springs. The street, otherwise, was lined with that curious anachronism on the California Coast, a series of black and white half-timbered Tudor buildings. They were charming, but they looked like stage sets.

The whole valley looked like a stage set. What was more remarkable, everyone seemed to be "doing his own thing," whatever it might be, and that included accepting her in her unkempt and tattered condition. It might be pleasant but it was also, in her experience, a trifle eery. As she passed the pretty Tudor overhangs on the story-and-a-half buildings, she found herself oppressed by the silence within. It was almost as if no one lived behind those nostalgic masks of old English houses built in a long line with only one wall between each unit.

The public parking lots seemed to be behind the buildings that lined the west side of the street. Through a short tunnel under a wing of the severely elegant Spa she could see that the vehicles in that lot behind the Spa were as varied in type as they were in license plates. Hong Kong and Buenos Aires were nestled up to elaborate cars with Arabic lettered plates and the lot, as she stopped to peer through the tunnel, was peppered with United States, United Kingdom, Pakistani, Swiss and Federal German Republic. There were also two cars of an old-fashioned solid build with Cyrillic lettered plates from Eastern Europe.

As Kay was returning through the little tunnel to the street, it occurred to her that some of the vehicles in the lot looked as though they hadn't been moved in months. Even years. Their owners must really have found their niche in the easy life of Lucifer Cove. She brushed herself off, sighed over her disheveled look, and went into the Spa next door to the tunnel. The entrance hall, while darkly elegant, did not impress her as quite the "incredibly rich" place that had been touted to her. The hall was narrow, dimly lit and when she passed a long-haired, healthy, suede-fringed pair —male and female?—they almost bumped into her, due, she hoped, to the indirect lighting.

Almost immediately, an open door on her left invited her into the reception room. She stepped into a tiny, beautifully funished room, all luxurious pink and gold, and subtly filled with a sensuous essence that even Kay, in her nervous, vengeful stage, felt to be highly contagious.

There was a bubbly blonde girl sitting at a dainty French First Empire desk, occupied with what appeared to be accounts in a large book covered with pink-figured brocade. Even the girl's ballpoint pen was pink. The girl looked up, bright-eyed, as Kay went to the desk.

"You just got to be Mrs. Aronson. We're lining up your appointments: Guiffredo's department at the Hot Springs for hair and facials. The sauna pool. Our fabulous dining salon. The Sea-Green Pool. Where do you wish to start, Ma'am?"

"I'm sorry. I don't wish to start anywhere at the moment. I'm here to . . . to live quietly for a time. I lost my husband recently. Are you Miss Bryer, the young lady who talked to me on the telephone an hour ago? That was most kind of you to call."

Bonnie Lou was all a-flutter.

"Nothing at all. Really, Ma'am. Your husband was one great guy. Generous? You can imagine. I didn't know him too well, but he was a doll. Had a first class hotline to the Spa's big boss too. Everybody doesn't get that."

"Really?" Kay metaphorically pricked up her ears. "Mr. Aronson and the 'boss' of this place knew each other well?"

"Oh, yes! Years and years. Way back when your husband was starting—at least, that's the story—he knew Mr. Meridon."

"Mr. Meridon?"

"Marc Meridon. He runs the Spa. I think he owns a piece of the Hot Springs, too." The girl shrugged and confided, "Not that I believe everything I hear. Marc couldn't very well have known your husband when Mr. Aronson was young. Marc's pretty young right now. But he's connected with your husband. Maybe Mr. Aronson got Marc started in business, or something."

"It must be something like that," Kay remarked thoughtfully. Was she already on to some small part of the secret she had come searching for? It seemed too easy. Yet the death of Leo Aronson, a great man, might somehow be involved with a wheeler-dealer like this Marc Meridon. Maybe they had a business secret in common. More likely, though, Meridon got his financial start from Leo and grew tired of the debt.

Bonnie Lou said, "You'll be wanting a maid-companion, your secretary says. He just called. Sounds groovy."

Very much surprised at this evaluation of the inhuman and impersonal Arthur Dugald, Kay agreed hastily. "He is a remarkable man. By the way, I wonder if I may see your Mr. Meridon sometime soon."

The girl blinked her big, heavily-made-up eyes, and looked around, as if about to impart some weighty secret. Her sexy voice hushed suddenly.

"Well, you'll be meeting him almost any time. Only he's out now. He comes and goes. It's really

47

hard to keep track of him. But you'll adore Marc—Mr. Meridon. All us femmes do."

The girl's excitement, her overenthusiasm, had the effect of prejudicing Kay against this paragon, Mr. Meridon. Either that, or the girl's nervous intensity. No question about her attachment to her boss. But why the nervousness? Why the quick glances around?

Or am I imagining mysteries, secrets, everywhere?

"I see. Thank you. And I would appreciate it if you would ask Mr. Meridon to give me a few minutes of his time when he returns. Meanwhile—I do need some repairs."

Bonnie Lou moved closer and looked her up and down.

"Been up at the Hot Springs in a love-in?"

Hardly knowing whether to be indignant or to laugh, Kay made a joke of it. "Not quite. More like a dog and cat fight. A big, light hound was killing one of the local pet cats, and I got in the middle."

"*Pet cat?*" The girl's voice went off-pitch so suddenly Kay stared at her.

"I suppose it's a pet. Poor thing. I was terribly sorry not to rescue the little cat. But it crawled away to . . ."

"Not to die, Mrs. Aronson," the girl protested with a peculiar and unexpected breathless quality. "Why, it just couldn't." She became aware of Kay's startled gaze and explained with a wild waving of arms: "Nine lives, you know. Kinkajou has—oh—lives he's never even touched yet."

"I hope so. I felt terrible. I don't know what happened to the hound, either. I hope his owner

48

recaptures him before he does more damage. I hate cruelty to anything so defenseless, so little." Kay thought over what she had just said. "As a matter of fact, I hate any kind of cruelty . . . especially to animals."

Bonnie rolled her eyes. "I know just what you mean, believe me. With people—so it's cruelty. But poor little fuzzy dogs and cats and birds, even mice. I hate to take a dead mouse out of a . . ."

"I understand," Kay cut in hastily. "Now, if I can change for a swim and have a hair appointment immediately after. Can someone come here to do my hair?"

"Sure thing. They do it a lot that way. When our customers—I mean our clients—can afford it. And most of them can, let me tell you." The girl giggled. "I guess that's not one of your problems, Mrs. Aronson."

Kay smiled. A lifetime had almost, but not quite, removed her self-consciousness and a childhood sense of guilt over her money. "Thank you. Do I sign?"

For some reason the girl was getting more and more nervous, or anxious. "Sorry, r-right here." She offered Kay a pink card with an elegant gold edge. "Name, address, birthdate, next of kin, preference of h-habitation . . ."

"I see." Kay filled out the required facts, omitting her year of birth, and arrived at "next of kin." The dainty pink pen was poised above the card. "Why must they have next of kin, for heaven's sake?"

"That? Oh—" Bonnie swung the card around and stared at it as if she had never seen it before.

"It's because so many people get to like it here and they stay and stay. When their money runs out, sometimes they work their way, here or at the Hot Springs. Take Edna Schallert. And young Caro Teague. They've been here for ages. Miss Schallert is rich, of course, but Caro works her way."

Kay put Arthur Dugald's name down after some deliberation. He would be the nearest person to the Spa, in case she had any accident or illness. It was risky, but everything she did here was risky. Then she looked up at a name pronounced by the girl. "I'd like to see Miss Schallert. She was at the chalet before my husband arrived. She is staying here at the Spa, isn't she?"

Vaguely, Bonnie Lou looked out the window behind her and then over Kay's head at the door to the hall.

"That's hard to say. She was going to stay here. She doesn't usually, though. She was feeling rotten about the suicide of her boy—a friend. That was just before your husband arrived. She got so sick she went to the Hot Springs sickbay—the clinic—before she packed up to leave the chalet."

"Just tell Miss Schallert when you see her that I'd like to have lunch with her sometime. Which is the way to the place they call the Sea-Green Pool?"

The girl swished her hips around the desk and walked with Kay to the entrance hall, pointing to the imposing but equally dark cross-corridor.

"To your right. Folks here kind of like their privacy; so I'll let you go on your own. End of the corridor and to the left. Doesn't seem to be anybody in the pool now. At least, I don't hear them. Probably all at lunch or in the Mirror Room Bar. That's beyond the pool on the far side. On the right end of the hall is that big staircase to the suites upstairs. Gorgeous suites. Just everything you could possibly want."

Kay thanked her and went along the hall. The first door to the right was ajar and revealed intriguing glimpses of a dainty Regency salon, white and gold with a soft restful pink patina over it all. Why the pink everywhere, she wondered, and decided it must be used for its therapeutic value. It had a flattering, soothing effect, and made all the women clients look younger.

The corridor itself was paneled with mirrors, a somber, elegant place, but made no less somber by the infinite reflections. A beautiful, tawny-haired woman about Kay's age was coming down the wide, depressing Jacobean staircase at the end of the hall and talking with a tall, lean-faced man whom the woman addressed as Dr. Rossiter. They were on the landing halfway down the stairs and obviously did not see Kay in the hall below.

"He is always in more danger on those occasions. I live in constant dread, Doctor."

"I should think there might be a great relief, Christine. Certainly, I needn't point out the relief of—of others at such a time."

"I don't think you quite understand me yet, Doctor. I love him. The other—the real one—whatever he is—makes no difference to me."

They were starting down the second flight of stairs to the hall below, toward Kay. Embarrassed at having been caught eavesdropping, she stepped into the deep shadow of the staircase as the pair continued to the hall. The doctor sighed. His voice began to fade. The two were moving rapidly down the hall, retracing Kay's steps toward the reception area.

"It is always the way. I suppose it has been true since the beginning of mankind. The devilish attraction of . . ."

Kay finished the thought herself: "The devilish attraction of some men." Thanks to her first two calamitous marriages, she had been able to appreciate Leo Aronson's quite different qualities. "No one will ever fool me again with a devilish attraction," she promised herself.

When the pair were gone, she crossed the hall to the double doors on the left. One wall here was of double glass decorated with exquisite pressed butterfly wings between the two thicknesses. She stepped into the great, high-ceilinged room beyond. The floors were tiled, a blue-green like the domed roof over the pool whose waters lapped pleasantly near her feet. There were echoes everywhere. The slightest sound was picked up, even the distant murmurs and laughter in a room beyond the far side of the pool, opening off a short, mirrored gold hall. On the left side of the little hall were dressing rooms and showers for those who used the Sea-Green Pool. The pool was empty now. Ideal for Kay's use, though a swim alone would not serve her purpose of making varied acquaintances here at the Spa. But it would soothe her tired and scratched body.

She walked around the pool and chose a dressing room, remarkably equipped, even to a choice of swim suits in the drawers of the built-in cabinets. Several of the maillots seemed to fit her as did the bikinis, and all appeared to be new and unused. Small wonder the charges at Lucifer Cove were so high! She undressed and showered while she wondered whom the beautiful, tawny-haired Christine and her Doctor Rossiter were discussing. Sardonically, Kay reflected that good health seemed to be the least of their goals here. And once again she wondered what, in particular, had been the Cove's fascination for Leo. Why had it been so necessary for him to visit the place at this time in his life when he was ill and such a trip might be dangerous? As, indeed, it had been!

She chose a plain black maillot without thinking about it and then found that it looked extraordinarily good on her, perhaps due to the juxtaposition of the stark black against her pale blonde hair and sunny gold skin. She felt guiltily pleased at her appearance in the full-length mirror on the inside of the door, before she stepped out onto the tiles above the pool steps.

The water was superb; the temperature exactly right. Not too warm and muggy. Not cold enough to produce gooseflesh. She walked around to the deep end, dove in, cutting the water neatly, and swam the length of the pool before she stopped to breathe deeply and to float, relaxed. She couldn't remember when she had last relaxed. It felt delicious. Momentarily no worries. No problems. Everything would work itself out.

The buzz of conversation and tinkle of glasses in the bar off the corridor reached her distantly. She heard something else then, the slight grating sound of a footstep on the tile. She looked up but the blue-green shadows, or the reflection of the rippling water, seemed to swallow the big room in shimmering waves. She blinked water out of her eyes, looked again. Nothing. She floated once more, but less calm and relaxed now that her mood had been broken.

Suddenly, water spurted out of the mouth of an idiotic stone dolphin perched dangerously near the diving board. The force of the water caught her in the face and she fell back, momentarily blinded, coughing and choking. She must have screamed, but she was aware only of the danger of losing consciousness, and she marshaled up all of her furious determination to stay above water. Even so, it was a struggle that took all her strength and began to terrify her.

Blindly, she scrambled through the deep water for the side of the pool, felt for it, found nothing. Her lungs were bursting.

Suddenly, a hand caught her groping fingers, drew her to the water-slick tiles that rimmed the pool. She blinked rapidly, and took long, cutting breaths as she tried to make out a figure in the blue-green shadows.

FIVE

Through the rippling layers of color that shrouded the area beyond the pool, Kay shook her head once more, spattering her rescuer with drops of water. Then she opened her eyes and tried again to see whose hand had saved her as she was partially lifted and partially pulled herself up onto the pool's tile edge.

She noticed his voice first. Quiet but oddly charming, with the faintest suggestion of . . . an accent? No. A brogue. At any rate, someone from a country foreign to this area.

"That was close. Some workman seems to have taken it upon himself to refill and clean the pool."

"And he nearly sent me down the drain." But she tried to laugh, to put a good, if wet, face upon her narrow escape. She looked up, blinked, and looked again into the face of her rescuer.

She was aware of his eyes first. Luminous dark eyes of extraordinary brilliance, yet shadowed and somber, she thought. She scarcely noticed the rest of his face until he himself released her from the intensity of his gaze by glancing around and giving an order to someone out of sight.

"Jeremy, that dolphin spout was turned on by mistake. See to it."

Kay studied him as he gave his quiet but perfectly audible orders. He appeared to be a slight man of middle height, no more, with dark hair worn a trifle longer than she was used to seeing on Leo or Arthur, or Leo's friends. A pale mouth, at once sensuous and reserved, and high, prominent cheekbones. He wore a jaunty scarlet-figured scarf in place of the tie she had expected, and she thought it very attractive against what appeared to be his natural pallor. He seemed to be under thirty. Much younger than she had expected to find Marc Meridon, and he must be Meridon. He was giving orders like a man used to command. As he turned his head, she saw a livid scar across his jawbone, partially concealed by his scarf.

He returned his gaze to her suddenly. Aware that she must have seemed very rude, staring at him, she tried to smooth her soaking wet hair, and began to get up.

"I really should be getting dressed. I'm late for lunch. And then—I have many things to do." She held out her hand. "I'm Kay Aronson, by the way. From the chalet."

He took her hand. "I know. I'm Marc Meridon. I hope you won't let this unfortunate business prejudice you against the Cove. We'll try and make it up to you."

"I understand you were a friend of Leo's. My husband, Leo Aronson." She found herself darting on verbally, although she knew perfectly well she did not suspect Marc Meridon of any wrong-

56

doing. That long, warm, questioning gaze of his was extremely moving. She found herself swayed by it in spite of her determination to suspect everyone, starting with Arthur Dugald and including everyone at Lucifer Cove.

"I admired your husband more than I can say, Mrs. Aronson. He was a brilliant man. He outwitted me, time and again, in our little business deals. But I've seldom known a man I admired more."

She pretended to have her mind on wringing water out of her suit, but she was very much aware when she said casually, with a little laugh, "I can't imagine your having deals over many years with Leo. Wasn't he considerably older than you?"

He smiled. "I learned a great deal about humanity from Leo—Mr. Aronson. He was very human, for a great man."

"I couldn't agree with you more." Without looking fully in his direction, she knew he was staring at her, that he observed her from the wet, straight length of her hair, over her still damp body, to her bare golden legs and feet. She had been studied before, and propositioned, and loved, and it was a long time since she had felt her entire body prickling with sensuous awareness of a man. She began to get up. "I must dress and have my hair done, and—" She laughed. "And eat. It suddenly occurs to me that I haven't eaten since dinner last night."

He was on his feet with an easy, almost feline lightness, and she found herself standing, with his hands lightly resting on her forearms. He withdrew them almost instantly. "May I introduce you to our dining salon?"

She hesitated. It was a perfect way to know him better, and to find out what he knew, if anything, about the plane crash and Leo's death. But some needling consciousness reminded her of the man's extraordinary and perhaps dangerously persuasive physical attraction. He must have misinterpreted her silence because he grew a trifle more formal, cooler. The knowledge that he had drawn away from her was annoying. She tried not to admit it was also disappointing.

"I beg your pardon, Mrs. Aronson. I imagine you prefer something more private. There is a rather charming little roof garden on the south wing, above the tunnel to the parking lot. You may have absolute privacy there."

"That would be delightful. With that blue sky out there, it's hard to believe we haven't gotten through January yet. A roof garden sounds exactly right." she knew she should be moving, walking along the tile bands to her dressing room. So far, disconcertingly enough, she hadn't moved a muscle, until he moved. She was disgusted at her own peculiar and unaccustomed weakness.

He began to stroll along the edge of the pool with her. "I'm afraid those blue skies won't last. We are too close to the coast. We'll be getting one of those salty white fogs by four o'clock. I hope you like fog."

She shivered. "It depresses me. It really does. I don't know why, except . . . Does it ever seem to you that one of those thick, smothering fogs is a little like being dead? A kind of shroud?"

He looked at her. She saw that she had startled him. "As a matter of fact, Mrs. Aronson, I've found death can come shrouded in a fog, or in rain, or at night . . . or under a very bright blue sky."

She asked abruptly, "Is that how Leo found it? Under a very bright blue sky?"

But he seemed to be ready for that veiled accusation.

"It was raining that morning. His plane took off against gusty headwinds. But I believe all that came out in the investigation."

"Yes. I'd forgotten." She was relieved to have reached her dressing room without insulting him further. She only hoped she hadn't completely aroused his suspicions of her motive in coming here.

He said as he was leaving her, "I'll send a hairdresser to you at once. When you are ready, someone will show you the way to the roof garden. You will find everything laid out there for your private dining. Ring for service."

"Thank you." She gave him her best smile, hoping for many reasons, that she had not completely antagonized him. She had to be content with the slightly formal smile that did not reach his eyes.

When she was alone, had showered and was wrapped in a commonplace but highly useful towel robe, the hairdresser, a skilled and sleek man named Guiffredo, arrived. He was accompanied by a preposterous old witch-like woman with grey locks shooting out all over her head, including her nostrils and ears.

"Mrs. Peasecod, dearie," this astonishing creature introduced herself. She brought with her a neat traveling wardrobe on wheels, and, what was more astonishing, every item in her magic wardrobe not only fitted Kay to perfection but was created in her most flattering colors.

Since she would be hiking up that mountainside trail quite a bit, Kay chose, among other outfits, a pair of close-fitted pants that indicated the long, slender shapeliness of her legs, and a long torso-knitted sleeveless sweater, belted in hammered gold, which she wore over a full-sleeved blouse.

Even the imperious Guiffredo confessed she looked "Exquisite. Truly that, Signora Aronson." And being thus inspired, he created an easy coiffure for her fine-spun, pale blonde hair, drawing it back and binding it at the nape of her neck with a leather thong. There were minutes when she surveyed herself in the long mirror that she entirely forgot the bitter purpose that had sent her to this place. She no longer looked like one of the richest women in America, or *Women's Wear Daily*'s figure on an easily demolished pedestal. She looked, to herself at least, exactly like any other good-looking, appealing young woman dressed spectacularly right in unspectacular clothes.

Payment to Guiffredo, Mrs. Peasecod, and a shy young midinette was to be made through the Spa which would get its bills from the Hot Springs. Kay did not think too much about it, but during that brief, casual explanation, she got the feeling that a single, powerful intelligence was behind the running of the entire Lucifer Cove.

She wondered whom it could be. Certainly, Marc Meridon was too young.

Or was he?

She had known people before who looked exceedingly young. Only their own worldly knowledge, their sophistication and experience revealed their true ages far more accurately than any facial lines so frantically massaged by the vain youth-worshippers of the world. Kay wondered about Marc. Though he looked no older than thirty, his perfectly free talk of relations with her husband suggested a man twice as old. Then she laughed. It was manifestly impossible.

Guiffredo had gone and the young midinette, looking soulfully at him, followed close after. Mrs. Peasecod stopped, however, for a last word with her new patron, breathing heavily and unpleasantly in Kay's face.

"Bear in mind, dearie, anything your little heart desires I got at my shop up the street. Not that they aren't broadminded here at the Spa. And I hear tell they can be way out up at the Hot Springs. If you're on the stuff—or just plain liquor—order up and it's there like that. Not that you'd be mainlining it. Not with that skin. But I just thought . . . Well, you never can tell when you need a little stuff specially cut."

"I don't," said Kay, trying hard not to show her revulsion.

"Well, then, sometime you might want something that'd remove any wrinkle, every little line—just about everything you could possibly dream of. Perfumes so musky, so full of aphrodisiacs you won't be able to crawl into bed except over bodies. Or . . . Well, anything else you got in mind. Just keep thinking of me, dearie."

"I certainly will." *I'll avoid you like the plague!*

Mrs. Peasecod waddled away, calling over her shoulder, "Don't forget. Anything. Clothes. Boots. Drugs. Cosmetics. Ammunition. Stuff to call up devils and junk. You know. Stuff for ectoplasm, it's called."

Cove clients were coming into the big Sea-Green room around the pool. Kay heard the echoes of laughter and teasing first. Most of the swimmers were youthful, but there were several potbellied, middle-aged men, and a couple of mature women who had obviously not gotten a good look at how they looked in their trunks and crowded bikinis.

Kay passed, trying not to let them guess her interest in them. Any one or more of them was a candidate for suspicion.

"No," she thought, after passing half a dozen youngsters. "Not these. Someone older. Older and in some way—probably business—connected with Leo. So far, the only one who seems to fit that category is Mr. Meridon." And she very much doubted that it could be Marc Meridon.

On the other hand, there was still Arthur Dugald. Now *there* was a mystery man. A good deal more mysterious and probably more dangerous than Marc Meridon!

She decided to banish suspicions, at least while she ate lunch. She met a young man near the reception desk who seemed to be stationed there especially to guide her up to the roof garden. She did not ask if Marc himself had stationed him there. They walked past an elegant pair of gold doors at the end of a corridor paneled with mirrors, and went up a flight of stairs at the back of the hall.

At the top of the small, unobstrusive white staircase above the second floor, Kay's guide threw open a green door onto a sunny rooftop, laced overhead with latticework and greenery.

"A skytop gazebo," Kay exclaimed, only half joking.

"For special clients," said the young man, with his hand on her forearm, attentively guiding her around a rather leggy planted tree in a long, rectangular planter. There was a coating of ashes over the surface of the planter and Kay was surprised that they didn't blow away, for there was a brisk, if pleasant breeze blowing in from the ocean. The tree looked like a stiff, Japanese miniature whose cultivation had taken place in reverse. There was a faint, gray cast to the needles. Was it actually a pine? But worst of all, its roots reminded her very much of a squid's tentacles, undulating over the ground through the pebbles and ashes of the planter.

"It's certainly large for an example of bonsai," she remarked, seeing that the young man had noted and was amused by her revulsion.

He looked the tree up and down. He seemed to admire it. The branches and needles were twisted in a southerly direction to lean over the patio, whether deliberately by man or by nature she couldn't guess, but when she sat down at the glass patio table she was very much aware of the tree's foliage and longest branches stretching over her head.

"Beautifully asymmetrical," he remarked.

When he saw that Kay was seated and apparently satisfied with the nicely modulated air and remarkably clear view, he added, "Would you care to order now? A cocktail first? Perhaps a 'Lucifer'?"

It sounded like something served in a Polynesian restaurant, served in a skull and adorned with floating gardenias so she smilingly refused it. "I will have a straight Scotch, in a schnaaps glass. Then I'll look over the menu."

"No champagne cocktail?"

"No. Just the Scotch. In one of those tiny Swedish glasses."

He was obviously having difficulty understanding this order and it amused her to see how the word "why?" trembled on his lips. The liquor idea was reasonable enough to him. He simply couldn't figure the importance she gave to the kind of glass. And she felt no necessity to explain that she had drunk this liquor in this manner at lunch for five years, every time Leo could take time out of his frenetic day for a private lunch with her. The schnaaps glasses had been what remained of his first present to her when he set out to convince her she might have better marital luck with him. Dear Leo!

There was a hot prick of tears behind her eyelids, and she looked up, blinking, pretending to find a fascination in the tree branches over her head.

"Of course. Exactly as you like it, Mrs. Aronson," the young man agreed, bowing slightly and leaving her, as she supposed, alone with her thoughts. She looked around at the Tudor rooftops across the little main street. No smoke curled around those chimney pots. Behind the Tudor row was a desert all the way to the eastern range, stony and dry, with an occasional gray-green plant and a few brave wildflowers, mostly mauve color. Odd to see wildflowers in January.

Along the west side of the rooftop the vista to the coast might have been better if there weren't quite so much white latticework which adjoined the busy greenery overhead. The southwest corner of the roof was completely in shadow, with another of those gigantic-miniature pine trees, or whatever the devil they were, hovering over some of the healthiest azalea plants she had ever seen.

She was dreamily, and pleasantly considering the remarkable uses of the California climate when the bush plants began to quiver with an energy that puzzled her. She was just thinking of going over to investigate the phenomenon when a husky voice, possibly female, called to her from that green jungle.

"This is my lucky day. Hi, there, Mrs. Aronson. Kay, isn't it? Any chance of my getting a teeny-weeny interview?" The body behind the voice popped out into the sunlight, freckled and scrubbed, a fiftyish woman with a lean, bony body revealed all too clearly in violet "hot pants" and a brief bra that was more than adequate for what she was covering.

Kay was still trying to refuse the request gracefully while retaining a reasonable amount of politeness when the woman took lanky strikes toward her.

"Thalia Cates of the McKesson Syndicate. We're negotiating for the A.P. When I get back in harness I hope you'll be reading my byline in the Class A sheets."

"How do you do, Miss—Mrs. Cates." Clearly, there would be no more gentle solitude or private lunch. Kay put the best face on it and asked Thalia Cates to join her for lunch. Unfortunately, Mrs. Cates accepted her invitation so quickly she almost snapped on the end of Kay's remark.

"Oh, this is really gorgeous. You're beautiful to do this, Kay. A beautiful person. Not the least like the newsies paint you." She was pulling out the white-painted metal chair opposite Kay, but her non-stop voice did not once run down. "What are you ordering, Luv? The Lucifers are sneaky. Kind of distilled LSD. And they're lethal. At this place you can get anything. But anything." Her narrow eyes, much more clever than her tongue, bored into Kay. "You tried any of the local delights yet? Just get hold of an old witch named— hold onto your girdle—Peasecod. There's nothing that old harridan won't get you. What would you like?"

Fortunately, Kay heard the young waiter arriving with the tray and her drink. As if the management of the Spa could read her mind, there on the gold tray was a tiny schnapps glass, about the size of a generous shot glass. It was the exact duplicate of the set Leo had given her five years ago. Rather an astonishing trick, to produce a glass identical to those others when they could not be common at American bars, nor were they much in demand, in Kay's travel experience. Beside the little glass was a pint-sized square bottle of her favorite brand of Scotch, and a little carafe of water. It seemed a great deal in order to give her one jigger of whisky, but she was impressed.

"They must be conjurers here," she murmured, staring at both bottle and glass. "How can they possibly guess so exactly?"

"Mind readers. Sneaky, sinister mind readers," Mrs. Cates remarked in sepulchral tones. She looked up at the expressionless waiter and winked. "Isn't that the truth?" But Kay saw the young man did not change his blank expression by so much as an eyebrow. He might as well have been a robot. Indeed, there were qualities about him that suggested some kind of carefully-put-together zombie.

"The Spa, I believe, has a well-deserved reputation for efficiency," he said, rather obviously addressing Kay.

"That's supposed to put me in my place," Thalia Cates assured Kay with a grin. She leaned forward over the table, as if the waiter were an invisible man and pursued her voracious curiosity.

"You here to build up to your next, Kay?"

Kay waited until the waiter had broken the seal on the bottle and left to get her a menu. Then, as she poured the pale amber whisky she asked innocently, "My next what?"

"Now, now, don't be coy with old Thalia. Just remember, we're all here for a reason."

Kay paused in the act of setting the bottle back on the tray. Sounds around them in the arbor, and overhead, the birds in the latticework all seemed to stop. There was a palpable silence, pregnant with meaning. No question about it, she thought. There were secrets here at Lucifer Cove.

Borrowing a little of the woman's effrontery, she studied Thalia Cates as she asked, "Do tell me. Why are you here? What is your reason? I'm sure it must be fascinating."

Instead of putting on an insulted or secretive air, the woman surprised her by positively twinkling.

"Fascinating isn't the word for it, believe me. Have you met the . . . well, I guess you'd call him the manager at the Spa? I think of him as Mr. Big."

Kay was belatedly aware of the little chill that invaded her body just when she thought she was immune to the pain of personal interests. "I don't think I know what you are getting at."

Thalia Cates batted her pale, sparse lashes.

"What I mean to say is, don't you find him fascinating? The man who manages the Spa? And would you believe it? He's just my type. Where else can you find a man my age who's my type? But there is . . . Marc Meridon."

This was so unexpected, and clearly such an aberration on Mrs. Cates' part, that Kay could only stare at her and repeat with a rude implication she couldn't control, "Marc Meridon is *your* age?"

Thalia Cates didn't take offense. "Oh, yes. He's exactly my type. Why? Did he strike you as your type? Believe me, Kay, all's fair in love et cetera. If you want to cut in, you've a perfect right to."

Kay submerged, with difficulty, the quick, angry retort that rushed to her mind and almost to her lips. No use in expecting that Thalia Cates' of the world to understand that such talk at the moment was like throwing mud on Leo's grave.

68

"I've met Mr. Meridon. I hadn't considered his age. To tell you the truth, I haven't given him much thought either way. I am a widow, after all . . ." She had a feeling she wasn't getting her point over. She let a little hardness creep into her tone. "He is all yours, Mrs. Cates. If that is what you are getting at."

Thalia became all flutter and feminine embarrassment. "You *are* a jewel, Kay-Luv. I really was getting to that. I saw him first, after all." She waited while the waiter laid the enormous, gold-medallioned menu beside Kay's hand.

"Try the eggs Lucifer." Her giggle grated on Kay's ears. "I think we're going to hit it off great. Just great. We do understand each other's territory."

Kay couldn't resist asking, "And what is my territory? Or rather, what do you think is my territory?"

"That," said Thalia leaning forward with a coy, fanning motion, "is precisely what I'd like to send out under an exclusive. You know. A Thalia Cates byline. In twenty languages. Twenty tongues, as they say."

Kay considered the enormous menu, the endless choices, and because of those choices, she discovered her desires to be surprisingly simple.

"Buttered cracked wheat toast. Apple juice. Coffee."

"And—?" The waiter hinted, holding his ballpoint gold pen poised above his gold-edged pad. Things went heavily to gold here. Either that, Kay thought cynically, or the billing would explain how they could afford it.

"That will be all, thanks."

"Jesus! That your idea of a lunch?" cried Mrs. Cates. Something about her objection caused the young waiter to stare at her, frowning.

The woman acted surprisingly subdued. Almost frightened, Kay thought, although she couldn't imagine what the woman said that was so shocking. The profanity was common enough, perhaps too common for the elegance of Lucifer Cove?

"Sorry," Mrs. Cates said quickly. "None of my business. Go on with your order, Jeremy."

Jeremy was going on, in any case, and Mrs. Cates' permission, too casually given, made him glance at the woman with a contempt that Kay found both puzzling and insulting.

When he had gone, Thalia Cates laughed self-consciously. "Well, well, well. I've a feeling you're to be treated specially. But don't press too hard. You may find nobody in this place has any real say except the—" She paused. Again, the self-conscious quality. "—the management, let's say."

Under the glass top of the table Kay could see her bony fingers working nervously. Almost at once, seeing Kay's curious glance, she got up abruptly and began to stride back and forth. Her stalking brought her closer and closer to the roof's edge. Along the east side of the roof garden there was a low white lattice fence about two feet high. She looked over that, down into the main street below and the black and white, half-timbered Tudor line of buildings across the street.

Kay watched her. She had not forgotten the woman's prying remarks, and in the intervening minutes she had found some questions of her own.

70

"Have you been here long, Mrs. Cates?"

The woman did not look around. "About three weeks. I've been dying to get my teeth into a really top assignment. Already, in three weeks, it's been coming true. This place is like that. It's in the air. Success. Believe me, it'll be worth it. In spite of that old Schallert woman. I swear, she's crackers!"

She took a sharp breath and, balancing herself carefully, leaned over the low latticework fence to see something—or someone—in the street below.

"Now, what the devil's he doing here?"

Kay, who had meant to ask about Edna Schallert, was sidetracked. "Someone you didn't know was here? This is such a small place. I should think everyone would know everyone else."

"But Luv, I haven't seen Adam Dulane for—why, it must be seven—maybe eight years. He was up to something with old Aristede Amanos in Detroit. I wonder who he's knifing in the Cove?"

"Knifing? What on earth do you mean?" Kay left the table and joined her just as Mrs. Cates was turning away from the roof's edge.

"I'd better go and tell Marc Meridon what I know about him."

"What you know?"

"What I suspect anyway. There was an attempt on old Amanos' life along about that time. Amanos was very big in one of those auto unions."

"You can't mean that a murderer is running around in this place!"

"Why not? Everything else is here? Or haven't you noticed, Kay?"

Curious in spite of herself, Kay was looking

71

down at the passersby when her heart seemed to turn over and then right itself, and she was aware of a numbing fear. A man across the street was strolling along studying with interest the buildings that marked the way. She recognized him as Arthur Dugald, but she had a dreadful feeling that Thalia Cates knew him under another name.

"Which one is Adam Dulane?" she asked, hoping against hope.

Mrs. Cates looked back at her casually. "That tallish, fair-haired chap across the street. Type that fades into the woodwork if you're not aware of him. But he doesn't fool me. See? He just looked this way. Yes. That fellow is Adam Dulane, all right."

The fellow was also Arthur Dugald.

SIX

Because Mrs. Cates had suddenly begun to look at her with an inkling of the truth, Kay was relieved to note the arrival of the waiter and went at once to sit down at the table again.

"You know," began the columnist suspiciously, "you act as if you were acquainted with ..."

"Are you intending to order?" Kay asked, and was infinitely glad to see her go toward the door in the wake of the waiter.

"Later. I really should warn Marc about that fellow. See you later, Kay." To the waiter she remarked with a degree of excitement, "I wonder where I'll find Mr. Meridon at this hour."

When she had gone, Kay began to eat, but she suspected the woman was simply looking for excuses to talk with the Spa's manager. It annoyed her so much she realized after some self-examination that she had been jealous of Thalia Cates' apparently old acquaintance with Marc Meridon. Under the circumstances, it was so preposterous for Kay herself to care, that she frowned and reminded herself severely. "You know nothing about this man. You've talked to him a mere ten minutes."

"But," the voice of persuasion reminded her, "he saved your life." Not really. Not literally, of course. It was highly unlikely that she could have drowned in the pool. She was an excellent swimmer. But it had been a very uncomfortable few minutes, and she had been in a panic. No question about it.

"Besides, he is younger than I am. Anybody can see that."

But was he, though? He was a mysterious creature. And she suspected he was far more brilliant than a man in his position was likely to be. She wasn't quite sure she liked the idea of his intelligence, or the peculiar notion she had that he knew more than he ought to know about Leo Aronson. The more he did know, the greater likelihood that he might have some motive for wishing Leo Aronson out of the way.

He admitted they had been business rivals. It was almost as if another voice reminded her of this clue that added fuel to her suspicion. Strange that in Meridon's presence she was so easily persuaded of his innocence.

She finished her lunch, surprised to find she had eaten the dark gold meat out of a papaya as well as the simple meal she had ordered. Nice of someone to include the health-giving fruit. Was it the idea of the chef? Or the waiter? Or ...

There I go again. Was it Marc Meridon's idea? Why can't I get him out of my thoughts? She knew the real suspect was Arthur Dugald, alias Adam Dulane, and surprisingly enough after her own suspicions, she was upset by this information about the man who had been such a close acquaintance for five years. She had never known him well. Leo himself saw to that. There was always a certain secrecy in their work together, but still, she thought now, it would be infinitely easier if Dugald could prove to be innocent of complicity in—or knowledge of—Leo's death.

What had Adam Dulane, alias Dugald, done in connection with that union chief in Detroit? Was he a murderer, that cool, competent man she had taken for granted as Leo's secretary and companion for the years of her marriage? It was even possible that Thalia Cates was wrong, that Arthur had nothing at all to do with the attempt on the life of the union leader.

But she was forgetting Leo's cleverness, his ability to ferret out phonies.

She also remembered that she had known a surprising sense of safety during the hour she spent in the chalet examining the oddities of the place. At all times she had been aware that if anything went wrong, shrewd, quick-witted Dugald, Leo's trusted companion, would save her. Even during her moments of suspicion, she had reminded herself that Leo trusted Arthur Dugald, and Leo was the best judge of character she had ever known.

But there was no denying Thalia Cates' nasty bit of evidence. This rooftop brunch had produced an important addition to Kay's original set of suspicions: Arthur Dugald very possibly was only one more alias for a very sinister man. On the other hand she had not, so far, found anything to bolster her suspicions of the Lucifer Cove management's involvement in the arrival, departure and death of Leo Aronson. All that showed up against Marc Meridon, for instance, was his long acquaintance with Leo.

A business acquaintance. And she was convinced that his death was due to some business connection. The old prickling suspicion reappeared in spite of all her efforts. Meridon did seem to know more about Leo than most of Leo's business partners knew. Logically, he should be under strong suspicion. But, of course, there was no proof. There was no proof that either Meridon—or that Jekyll and Hyde, Arthur Dugald—had anything to do with Leo's mysterious and abrupt plane flight, much less his nightmarish screams.

But now Kay was too nervous to remain here and enjoy the roof garden's quiet beauty. After several minutes of attempting to sit calmly drinking coffee, she left the table, glanced up at the twisted tree overhead, and, without examining the rest of the little roof garden, went over to the door and started down the stairs.

Still wondering about the possible double identity of Dugald, Kay was startled to see the secretary striding along the second floor below her. She ducked back up through the green door and onto the roof, wondering at her own cowardly retreat. But she wasn't at all sure how she would handle her ambiguous relationship with Arthur Dugald in the future. No use in letting him guess what she felt yet, and she hadn't had time to compose herself after Thalia Cates' testimony about him.

She heard his step on the stairs and gasped. There was no avoiding the confrontation, just when she needed more time. And then, miraculously, she heard a man's voice calling to him from somewhere behind him on the second floor. Recognizing, or thinking she recognized Marc Meridon's voice, she went back onto the stairs, being careful not to betray herself, and was able to overhear his conversation with Arthur just out of her sight in the hall below.

"Good afternoon, Mr. Dugald. Were you looking for Mrs. Aronson?"

"As a matter of fact, I am. To escort her back to the chalet if she is ready. Or to be of any help to her here in the village if she wants anything. The chalet needs a few items."

"I'm afraid you just missed her. When she finished lunch she went out to examine the main street and probably the Hot Springs."

What a cool, fluent liar Marc Meridon was! And why did he go to this trouble to protect her from a man who would be living in the same house with her during her stay at the Cove? However, she thought she might thank him for his help when she met the Spa's manager again.

Arthur Dugald hesitated. "I see. One of the waiters told me I would find her in the roof garden."

So he knew about the roof garden! Had Dugald been here before? Or was he just repeating what he had learned from the employees of the Spa?

Marc said, "She was here I believe, a short time ago, Mr. Dulane. You will probably find her easily enough on the street or in Mrs. Peasecod's shop on the way to the Springs. The shop is the one with the Regency front and the oriole window."

There was a little pause while Kay held her breath with surprise at Marc's betrayal of suspicion. Thalia Cates must have gotten to him with her information. Anyone who didn't know Arthur Dugald would have thought he sounded quite normal, but to the ear of a woman like Kay who had heard him at all hours for five years, there was a note of strain in his voice.

"I beg pardon. The name is Dugald."

"Of course. Did I mispronounce the name? My memory! Or possibly I have you confused with a chap I once saw—I didn't actually know him—in the Midwest sometime during the early Sixties."

Marc was playing his cards close. Kay found his methods a little frightening.

The secretary, however, was now better able to handle himself, though Kay suspected from her knowledge of him that he had been thrown by Marc's unexpected attack.

"Probably you did see me. It would be hard to imagine a city I haven't been in, at one time or other."

"You come highly recommended, Mr. . . . Dugald. I won't keep you. I have already distracted you from your—shall we say—your destination?"

"You may say anything you like, sir. The Spa is yours, I believe," and Dugald's footsteps receded down the hall.

Kay considered with some ironic amusement that Arthur Dugald had gotten the last word against a man she suspected of being very clever himself. She waited uneasily until she was sure

78

the secretary had left the second floor, and was debating whether she should start down the stairs when she was startled to hear a well-remembered, charming voice with a trace of laughter:

"You are quite safe to come down now, Mrs. Aronson."

She tried to cover her embarrassment as she descended, pretending a complete self-possession she was far from feeling.

"Thank you. I wonder how you knew I wanted to avoid my husband's secretary. For the moment, at least."

Marc Meridon stood at the foot of the stairs and held his hand out to her. His fingers closed lightly over her own. She was aware of a certain excitement in his touch, in spite of an unexpected chill about his fingers. Perhaps he wasn't quite well, although she doubted that. There was something about the position of his thin fingers that suggested reserve strength, a very real strength quite at variance with the pallid, slender young man he appeared to be.

"Would you care to see the rest of the Spa? I think I can promise you we won't see your Mister—ah—Dugald on the grounds."

"Don't misunderstand me, Mr. Meridon. Arthur is the nearest . . . associate I have. He was my husband's closest confidant."

"Except yourself."

"No, no. Including myself. There was a great deal about Leo's business that I knew nothing about. I hadn't the head for it." As he looked at her she confessed with a smile and a little shrug. "I haven't the head for it yet. That is why Arthur is so necessary to me. But I like to escape him, now and then, the way . . ."

He laughed lightly. She felt that he understood. "The way a student escapes her master?"

"Her teacher," she corrected him.

"Of course."

She cleared her throat, began to speak, but was afraid to question him about the mysterious Adam Dulane without betraying something of her reasons for being here at Lucifer Cove.

"Yes?" he pursued gently. "May I help you in any way?"

She looked at him, at his eyes, almost as if she were willed to do so. She thought she had never seen eyes so luminous, so dark and passionately sincere. She wondered at her own original mistrust of him. She felt now that she could betray her suspicions of anyone to him, that he would help her, or at least give advice and sympathy. His sensual touch seemed now an aberration on her part. He was boyish, endearing. She stared at him, and burst out.

"Who is Adam Dulane?"

The same honest gaze was fixed on hers and it was hard to remember the conversation she had overheard between him and Arthur Dugald.

"I don't think I understand. You aren't thinking of your husband's secretary, Dugald?"

Was he merely being discreet over Dugald's affairs? Or was he—in spite of those honest eyes—a liar?

"Yes. As a matter of fact, I am referring to Arthur. Your client, Thalia Cates, told me she knew him in Detroit as Adam Dulane. Do you think that is possible? And if it is, once more may I ask, who was this Dulane?"

He smiled. "To tell you the truth, I'm afraid my source is the same as yours. Mrs. Cates is a very—"

"Talkative?"

"Gossipy, chattering woman. But out of those acres of chatter, she occasionally reveals something of interest. Immediately after she spoke to you in the roof garden she came down to report her discovery to me."

"You mean she told you all about Arthur's Detroit history? I must know. I really must know!"

They had passed a number of suits, one of which had the foyer door open, and Kay was vaguely aware of beautiful decor, blue Chinese silk screen walls and a great deal of luxury. Luggage was being carried out by one of the handsome young bellmen. She wondered what client was leaving and would have asked Meridon, but he seemed not to notice.

"I assure you I mean nothing except that Mrs. Cates warned me to watch Leo's secretary, that he was the Dulane chap who once worked for Aristede Amanos some years ago. Amanos has died, since, and I myself have heard nothing against this Dulane, or as a matter of fact, against Mr. Dugald."

"Then I suppose it is safe to have him in the chalet during my stay here?"

By this time the afternoon was well advanced and Kay, completely confused by all of the day's developments, made her excuses and left Marc Meridon outside the reception room, although he was very persuasive in asking if he might show her around the Spa. At the last minute he stopped her as she was leaving.

"Shall we send up one of our young ladies to act as your maid, or your companion?"

"Please. Either or both."

"Anyone in particular?"

"No. I leave that to you." But she wondered what sort of woman he would send. She thought she might learn a little more about Marc Meridon's own sincerity from the person he sent. She had expected a great many unpleasant developments in her search for the truth about Leo's death, but she hadn't imagined that one of her greatest difficulties would be the desire to believe in two men, either of whom might very possibly have engineered Leo's murder.

"Good. Then, Mrs. Aronson, we will send—I think—a young lady named Carolyn Teague within the next hour. She was about to be put in the dead file . . . that is to say, the inactive file, when this possible position became available. About your meals, you understand that meals can be taken to your chalet and reheated." She nodded tiredly. The confusion of her suspicions, versus a totally unexpected desire to find the men innocent, had come too soon after the shock of Leo's death.

"Send up your Miss Teague, and I'll consider the matter of my meals later."

Marc put his hand out and after a brief moment of surprise, she put her own hand into his. She felt herself shiver, whether at the cool touch of his flesh or at the undeniable power of the man's personality she didn't know herself. She was careful not to look at him, but went out to

82

meet a vigorous, salty wind blowing in from the coast. She was sorry to see that Marc had been right in his prophecy. Long lines of fog were propped in close battle formation beyond the western line of mountains. The entire Cove would be shrouded in fog by nightfall. She pulled her bright new fringed jacket around her and hurried along the street toward the gulley and the trail up the mountain.

As she passed the Tudor buildings with their curious, hollow, unlived-in look, like movie props on a back lot, she was suddenly reminded of a matter that had nothing to do with all these interesting scenic effects.

Where was Edna Schallert?

Why didn't I think to ask that talkative gossip Mrs. Cates about her? Certainly the sharped-eyed Thalia would know, if anyone did. Anyone except Marc Meridon, of course.

And I missed the chance to speak with him about a great many things. But especially about Miss Schallert. Yet the woman's ghostly presence seemed inescapable in the chalet. More particularly, when Kay remembered the woman's two lovers and their fates during a period of less than a year.

She went up the trail with surprising ease, considering how tired she had been. But there was no doubt of it. Her two encounters with Marc Meridon had invigorated her. Even though she wasn't sure of him, of his guilt or innocence, she recognized his effect on her as a woman. And he had seemed to be attracted to her. She wondered if there were any women seriously involved in Marc's life. There must be, of course, women like

Thalia Cates, with a juvenile crush on him and a fastastic misconception of everything about him, starting with his age.

Kay ducked under the low, groping branches of the cypress trees that hovered at the turn in the trail, and was reminded, for no reason, of Arthur Dugald. If he were innocent, why the name change? Added to this, all she knew or suspected about him since Leo's death made her wonder why she felt this terrific depression at the thought that her search for Leo's killer might soon be ended—in the person of Arthur Dugald, alias Dulane.

She decided it would not be safe tonight to sleep at the chalet without once again, and more thoroughly, checking the mountain cabin itself, including the cellar and that dark bedroom against the mountainside in which two dead men had slept, though at different times. Not the most salutary sleep, surely!

She would like to ask Edna Schallert some questions about the place and even, if possible, about the other bedroom and Miss Schallert's dead lovers. It would certainly pose a problem, but if Edna Schallert really was a woman in her late forties or fifties, she would not be coy and maidenly. She might even know what had happened to Leo during the brief time he had been at the Cove. Could the Schallert woman possibly have a clue to what made Leo leave Lucifer Cove in such a hurry?

The bushes, mesquite and brushwood, rattled their tight, dry foliage in the wind, reminding Kay of the sickening dog and cat fight she had witnessed early in the day. She moved off the trail just in time to appear as though she were making way for that triumphant priestess of the devil, Nadine Janos. The priestess was gliding along, all black and white fluttering draperies that floated around the slim Grecian column of her body.

"What the devil are you looking for?" she asked Kay, stopping abruptly and staring at her.

Kay looked around among the bushes.

"Gruesomely enough, I'm looking for a dead body, and rather hoping I don't find one."

Nadine Janos' composure, for once, was badly shaken. "Dead body! What's happened?" She hurried across the path, her prominent, smoky blue eyes staring fixedly at the ground as if she literally expected to find a body.

It was necessary to cut off this panic at once. The half-joke had backfired. Kay said quickly, "Only a cat. A likable little striped tabby." At the frozen expression on the priestess' face, she felt even more guilty. "Was he your cat?"

"N-not exactly. But are you . . . it can't be! Have you checked down in the village?"

She was acting as if the bottom of her world had fallen out. What was this thing Nadine Janos had for cats?

"No. I forgot to mention it. You see, he may not be dead. Only badly injured. But at any rate, it didn't occur to me to bring up the subject. You must know how it is at the Spa. I met a gossip columnist. I nearly drowned. I discovered some disquieting things."

"You nearly drowned! At the Cove?"

That, at least, took the priestess' thoughts off the fate of little Kinkajou. Embarrassed at having made so much melodrama out of a simple accident on the part of a Spa employee, Kay explained quickly, "Not actually a drowning. Or rather, I was rescued by the young manager of the Spa, Mr. Meridon. Just a matter of having a dolphin faucet turned off. Anyway, you can see I was too busy to . . . what is it?"

The young woman had suddenly blinked and began to look as if she were coming out of a stupor.

"Nothing. How was Mister . . . how was Marc? Friendly, or course, in his way. But I had the impression he'd been—ill. How did he strike you?"

Kay wondered what the interest of the priestess could be in Marc Meridon. Nadine didn't have the girlish crush on him that Mrs. Cates exhibited, but there was something, some keen, even violent interest.

"Mr. Meridon was charming. I take it that everyone—every woman at the Spa—thinks so. Would you say so?"

Nadine seemed about to ask something, hesitated, then said in a flat, expressionless voice, "Well, you can take it that every woman at the Spa thinks about him. Now, what about that animal?"

Kay shrugged. "I'm afraid the poor little thing must have crawled off to die. Its neck was badly mangled."

"No, no! The dog. What kind of dog was it that attacked Kinkajou?" Nadine was standing on the toes of her high-heeled, old-fashioned shoes, hitting at the bushes as if she expected to battle the ferocious dog with her bare hands.

Kay described the hound and was surprised at what she considered Nadine's offbeat comment.

"Now, I wonder what a liver-colored hound could be . . . really?" When she caught Kay staring at her, she said quickly, with a grin, "I know. Don't tell me. He could be a bad-tempered, liver-colored hound. But I don't recall ever seeing him in this part of the valley before. And to be quite frank, I'd as soon not meet him ever."

Kay heartily agreed with her. They separated and went their own ways. However puzzled Kay might be, she was interested to note that the priestess too had found something about their encounter confusing. She stopped twice on the way down the trail, looking out over the shrubs and then back in Kay's direction.

Kay sighed, rubbed one thigh whose muscles were definitely pulled by all this hiking, and went on to Leo's chalet, giving some thought to and more than one glance at Nadine Janos' white temple. The central doors were wide open. A tall, loose-limbed man with the map of Ireland on his likable face was busy hanging black drapes over the long windows inside. The windows were shuttered, so Kay supposed all the black material was merely for effect; to give the proper atmosphere.

Wondering whether she should go up now and ask to be shown through the temple, she had almost done so when she noticed movement on the porch of the chalet a quarter of a mile beyond. It seemed to be Arthur Dugald. What had he done? Run up the trail to be ahead of her? Or was there another way up here, a way she did not know about? Kay looked from the temple to that distant chalet and decided she couldn't let Dugald think he had intimidated her, that, in fact, she was afraid to encounter him.

Kay walked on just as the tall Irishman looked out at her curiously.

"And a good day to you, my lass."

She waved to him, amused by the brogue, unable to resist the friendly quality of his grin.

"Top of the mornin' to you, Sir."

By the time she reached the chalet, Arthur Dugald was still standing there, looking rather oddly down over the steep mountainside to the village below.

"Hello," Kay greeted him, relieved that she seemed more composed than he was. Besides, she was still set up by the Irishman's greeting of "my lass." "Admiring the fog banks? They will be up here any minute."

He looked at her, smiled, but with a bit of strain. "No, I keep seeing some kind of an animal down there among the sage and those weeds."

She started, unable to conceal her nervousness, and she was afraid he saw it. "If you mean Kinkajou, the cat, he was injured in a fight earlier today. He may have crawled off to lick his wounds."

"I think this is too large for a cat. At any rate, a domestic cat. I'd say it was a huge brown dog."

"A light, liver-colored hound? He's the one who almost killed Kinkajou." She didn't see the creature among the underbrush and didn't know whether she wanted to or not. If he was seen, he might be captured, which was all to the good. But on the other hand, selfishly, she would like to believe he had left the valley and was larruping along the coast toward a town with a large animal shelter and an active dogcatcher.

"Strange," Arthur Dugald murmured.

She looked at him. "How in particular?"

"What did he make you think of?"

She didn't know. "Danger, I suppose. I don't want him to kill the cat. Or me. What did he make you think of?"

"Death. . . . I'm probably thinking about Mr. Aronson. But I've always thought of death as a—never mind," He broke off so suddenly she stared at him.

She was more angry than frightened. It seemed so obvious, this cheap, shoddy attempt to alarm her.

"Well, I'll leave you out here with your deadly dog, while I finish unpacking and look over the house."

"If there is anything I can do to help . . ."

She was ashamed of the snappishness in her answer. "You can capture your precious dog of death, if that's your bag."

She went into the chalet. The lower floor was still dark, still curiously depressing, probably due to the contagion of Arthur's talk about death dogs. There was nothing dead in here. There was not going to be anything dead in here, if she kept her wits about her. But she couldn't get his fiendishly expressive picture out of her mind.

SEVEN

Kay was too nervous to take it easy, to rest or change or finish unpacking. She walked around the curious, circular room, examining the dark fireplace and pushing the door open to look in on the kitchen. There were certain feminine aspects to the kitchen, a set of embroidered place mats neatly done in an old-fashioned cross-stitch, piled on the little formica table top in one corner.

She was about to inventory a set of electric appliances on a long, handy sinkboard next to the refrigerator, when she saw a quick, blurred movement out of one of the back windows. The kitchen was very near the steep slope of the mountainside with its heavy undergrowth, but there was a small, intervening space and the afternoon sun slanted through the window in a cheerful way, just beginning to be pushed out of place by the rolling fog. She had a feeling that what she had seen on the mountainside was a dog, leaping from one concealing clump of brush to another. But she refused to fall into the trap that Arthur Dugald might be setting up, hoping that she would become increasingly frightened, sensitive to any suggestion by her possible enemies.

Arthur's voice from the living room doorway made her jump in spite of herself.

"All that electrical equipment doesn't look as though it was used very much. Good Lord! Even an egg poacher. That hardly seems Mr. Aronson's sort of equipment."

"He was only here a day or so. He may have eaten in the village."

The secretary shook his head. "Not according to anything I've learned. He was here one afternoon and night. His pilot stayed in a town on the other side of the mountain. Mr. Aronson saw only one person of any consequence from the Cove."

With a sick little prescience of the answer, she asked, "Who was that?"

"The fellow who calls himself Marc Meridon. They talked for a couple of hours."

"Did they quarrel?"

He looked at her oddly, his cool blue eyes curious, as if they would read her mind.

"Did you have reason to expect them to quarrel?"

Forgetting discretion, she asked querulously, "How else can we explain the way he left here so secretly, and then was—"

"Murdered?"

She stared at him, managed to recover herself and after quickly flicking her tongue over dry lips, she countered, "What on earth makes you think that? We've no proof. The investigation made it clear there was some malfunction. Some mechanical failure."

"It isn't unheard of for mechanical failure to be induced by human agency."

She tried to laugh. "Boiling that down to plain English, you would say someone here at the Cove wanted my husband dead?"

He actually grinned in a way that made him look suddenly very young, very comfortable to be with.

"Sorry. I'm afraid I've taken on the veneer of all the poorly educated, polysyllabic men I've . . . worked for." Just for an instant he paused. Obviously he intended to use another word and had remembered at the last minute that he must not betray—what?

She walked around the room, looking at the apparatus, the furnishings, found almost nothing that looked like a sign of her husband's having lived here.

Arthur Dugald remarked suddenly as he fingered an electric waffle iron, "I wonder if you wouldn't understand this better than I do."

Curious, she said, "Try me."

"Does it seem logical to you, Mrs. Aronson, as a woman, that this Edna Schallert should have left all her kitchen gadgets behind when her lease ran out?"

Kay looked around. There was a sandwich grill further along the board. And a broiler-fry pan. And, of course, a heating tray. Numerous other objects. All the things the woman obviously found indispensable. As Kay fingered them, she saw that they were much used. A trifle stained. Well scrubbed, though with steel wool that had left scratches.

"Yes. I agree. She evidently used these a great deal. I wonder why she didn't . . ."

He was looking into the cupboards, investigating odds and ends. One of the cupboard doors closed with a clatter. Both he and Kay jumped, then glanced at each other and laughed. He apologized ruefully.

"Sorry. I'm afraid there is a certain tension in the air. I can't speak for you, of course, Mrs. Aronson, but I'm constantly aware of something strange here in this valley. I keep thinking back to Mr. Aronson's nightmares."

"How could they be affected by this place?" She laughed but without humor. "Is it your idea that they used some remote-control business to scare him? Leo was not easily scared, you know."

"I don't know. To tell you the truth, I still think if we knew what caused those nightmares, we'd know a great deal more about his death."

She looked at him for a long time. He seemed entirely sincere. Still, how could one know for sure? She glanced out the window, frowned at the gathering overcast sky and motioned for him to leave the kitchen with her. They walked through the living room, and with his help Kay opened each shutter. The northern sky seemed to hurry in, sending long gray bars of foggy light across the floor. The room, more easily seen now, presented the forlorn look of a deserted ski lodge, with its great blackened fireplace and the worn furniture.

"Now. One more window and we'll have the west wall looking less gloomy," Kay suggested cheerfully as Dugald pushed open the warped shutter. But she was caught by the sudden sharpening of his expression as he turned and looked across the room toward the west wall.

In spite of his expression his voice was controlled and calm. "I could have sworn I turned off that television set early today."

She stared at the big, clumsy console, and for a few seconds couldn't see what he was talking about. Gradually, the dot of light in the center of the convex face of the set became visible.

"How odd! It makes me think of—of what?"

Dugald hesitated. "Have you ever studied the pupils of a cat's eyes, the remarkable way they dilate, or narrow to slits of light . . . like that?"

She burst into laughter that had a slightly hysterical edge. "Arthur, are you an animal hater? You do have a real thing about them! Watched by a cat! How do you like that?"

He said nothing but went over and examined the television set, snapped it off and on, studied it. He had laid the palm of his hand over the back of the set and when Kay joined him, beginning to suspect he had lost his mind, she was even more sure of it.

He raised his hand from the console and said one word which made absolutely no sense: "Cold."

"Should it be otherwise?"

"Yes, if it has been on since we were here this morning."

She stood back, studied the convex face of the set. "But it wasn't on, and it isn't on. It probably hasn't been on since I saw you turn it off hours ago. Really, Arthur, you are making a mystery out of the most ordinary, mechanical . . ."

There was a vague, almost shadowy face of

some kind peering at her from that blank television screen. She exclaimed something breathlessly and leaped backward. It was a horrid second or two before she recovered herself.

"Well?" he prompted her.

She laughed but couldn't disguise the nervousness in that laugh.

"Don't you see? It's our faces! Either yours or mine. We come near and our faces are reflected on the dark screen like a mirror."

"My dear Kay . . ." They were both so busy with their mystery they didn't notice his unaccustomed familiarity with her name. "That face may conceivably be mine, I don't know. I'm no judge. But emphatically, it is not the face of a beautiful woman."

She did notice the compliment and was moved by it. It had the added weight of being said almost without thought, a spontaneous and therefore more valuable thing. Her glance thanked him, but in that short space of time something had happened. Their haunted television set now appeared normal and blind: a dull, shadowed screen that did faintly reflect the room around them.

"You see?" she pointed out triumphantly. "Nothing at all. No ectoplasm. No cat's eyes. Not even your friend, the hound."

Reluctantly, he smiled and agreed. As she took another step away from the set she stumbled over an obstacle just off the carpet and said, "Damn! What's that?"

He had caught her before she fell and let her go almost without her awareness. He pointed out the clasp lock on the cellar door just as she saw it.

"I'm curious about that place," she said thoughtfully. "I'd like to know how deep the cellar is at the bottom of those steps."

With a haste that surprised her he said, "Forgive me, Mrs. Aronson, but I don't think it would be wise for a woman to wander around down there. It may be larger than we think. It may be much more than a cellar. The caves over the eastern range, near Hollister, wind through an entire mountain. However, with your permission, I thought I might take an examination some time soon."

She touched the lock with the toe of her shoe.

"I had no intention of going alone. I would certainly go down there with someone trustworthy." They both knew she was waiting for him to suggest that they make the examination together, but he said after an awkward pause.

"I was thinking of the insects. The spiders. And probably there are a good many rats. And then, it would be easy for a woman to stumble over the broken pavement, the rocky floor."

She had a burst of impatience and resentment that was very close to anger. "I am not, by nature, a stumbler. I stumbled just now because of this idiotic wooden door which has no business being set into the living room floor. Why isn't it out beyond the kitchen, like any self-respecting cellar ought to be?"

He laughed at that. "Because at the foot of those cellar steps, and to one side, is what remains of a cord of firewood. This sort of place is often handy to a fireplace, to protect the wood in case of heavy rains. And contrary to what you may have heard, it occasionally rains in these California mountains."

"Well, it is my cellar, after all, and if I want to go down into my own cellar, I will!" But the ultimatum sounded more than a little childish when she heard it spoken aloud.

In the voice of one soothing that unruly child in a temper tantrum, he said quickly, "and so you shall. I only suggest that you let someone else go down first and see if there are lights, and so on."

Somewhat mollified, she gave up both the cellar lock and the television with the life of its own, and started up the circular steps to the rooms above. She looked back, unsure what his plans were, half afraid he might leave her to her own devices in this very odd mountain house and half afraid, too, of his presence if he did share the place with her. When she leaned over the twisted metal rail to watch him she thought his tall, lean back was slightly ominous, his shoulders and build stronger than she had supposed them to be. Odd that she had never noticed this quality during the five years he worked for her husband.

Then, after studying the cellar lock for a minute or two, he turned around and, as if conscious that he was under close scrutiny, he looked up. Just for a second or two she thought with satisfaction, he had been startled by her intensive stare. His eyes were far more attractive, now that they were startled, than she found them usually, with their cool blue depths so very confident and without emotion.

"May I help you, Mrs. Aronson?"

"Since we will be sharing the same roof for

97

some days, you may as well call me Kay," she told him, making up her mind suddenly.

"Thank you, Mrs. Aronson. I might take the couch over under those two windows. It appears to be a studio couch. Then, if there are any—interruptions—I'll be handy to filter them through before they reach you upstairs."

"Are you expecting interruptions?"

"I'm expecting—I don't quite know. I wonder if you would do me a favor." He came to the bottom of the steps and started up toward her. She waited for him.

"I imagine so. What favor is it? Do you want the evening off?" She had meant it as a joke but it sounded unpleasantly patronizing when it came out. He reddened slightly and his mouth tightened as if he might be suppressing a very tart answer. She added quickly, "I'm sorry. That wasn't funny. It was a stupid thing to say."

His smile re-enforced her belief that in spite of Thalia Cates' gossip about him, he was, somehow, being sincere with his late employer's wife.

"I'm not sure Leo Aronson's wife could not be stupid," he said quietly.

She laughed. "What a whopper that is, Arthur! You really are too polite. Tell me," she went on as they walked up the steps into her bed-sitting room together. "What is this favor you want?"

"I would like to be sure, for your own sake, that you don't confide in anyone who comes from down there in Lucifer Cove."

"Anyone at all?" she repeated, wondering if he was afraid she would find out about the other man Thalia knew, Adam Dulane of Detroit who might, or might not be Arthur Dugald's Mr.

Hyde. "What about the guests there? I had a gossipy time this morning with a woman named Cates. A columnist, I believe." She tried to retain a bland, innocent expression, and hoped he didn't note the sharpening of her gaze as she watched him.

It was difficult to tell whether the name meant anything to him or not. He reminded her earnestly, "But we can't be sure these clients actually are strangers. Some of them—most of them, to judge by their cars in the parking lot—seem to spend the rest of their lives here."

"Surely, there is no harm in the workers, though. The waiters, receptionists, chambermaids. Because we will be having them here in the chalet, and they are bound to overhear some things said in confidence."

"Anyone, Mrs. Aronson. I meant—literally—anyone!"

At one of the windows she swung around from her view of the fog-shrouded valley below and demanded with a bluntness that surprised herself, "What are you afraid of? Why all this secrecy? Tell me honestly, Arthur, why do you think I should care about secrecy? I have no secrets."

He said coldly, "Haven't you?" And before she could get indignant, he looked down the spiral steps, waving her to silence. Then he crossed the room to join her at the window. His normally quiet voice had scarcely changed as he spoke, but she understood the danger that they might be overheard. "I know why you are here. I only wonder if the whole of Lucifer Cove knows as well."

"I am here solely because . . . what is it?"

He shook his head. "I thought I heard the front

door open, but it seems to have been my overactive imagination. You need not tell me why you came to the Cove. Or why you weren't satisfied with the verdict on the crash." She opened her mouth, then closed it abruptly. He smiled at her expression. "Aren't you going to ask me how I know?"

"I'm beginning to suspect. You weren't satisfied with the verdict either." She stopped, trying to identify an unexpected sound. Vaguely, it made her think of walls creaking and crackling with temperature changes. A little, crackling sound. "Someone really is downstairs!"

"Either that," he remarked dryly, "or these walls are older than we thought."

He glanced out the window. "Whoever it is, he left no friends outside." He started to the circular steps as she realized for the first time that those open steps were going to haunt her every night she slept here in the chalet.

"Find out who it is before you go down," she whispered, following him to the steps on the theory that he might need a little backing.

She couldn't see whatever it was that he saw as he started down and it was with considerable relief and impatience at her own fears that she heard Arthur Dugald say in his calm, emotionless secretarial tones.

"Good afternoon. Are you the young lady who is going to work for Mrs. Aronson?"

A soft voice answered him so quietly that Kay couldn't hear it. She started to go down the steps, attempting to pass Dugald but he put his arm out in a possessive, masterful way that would have

100

angered her at any time before the peculiar half-conversation the girl's entrance had interrupted.

"Please. Let me take a good look at her first," he told Kay in a low voice. She nodded and he went on down.

It didn't seem strange to take orders from Arthur Dugald, once she thought of it. During her entire marriage he had always been a kind of shield between the Aronsons and the outside world. He was still acting in that capacity, she hoped.

So much for the dirty, gossiping suspicions of Thalia Cates, a woman who was doubtless just as wrong about Arthur as she was about her intimacy with Marc Meridon, and Kay was confident that at this very minute the woman was down there in that fogbound little village, spreading tales about her "Luv" and bosom friend, Kay Aronson.

"Mrs. Aronson?" Arthur called from the lower floor. "The young lady is here, Miss Carolyn Teague."

"Please, everyone calls me Caro," said the girl as Kay descended to meet her. They shook hands while Kay looked her over, impressed by the basic beauty of fine-spun, red-gold hair and good facial bone structure. So much could be done with such a pretty face and so little had been done, it was surprising. The girl looked positively haggard, her large hazel eyes haunted and sad, and she appeared to be in a highly volatile state of nerves.

"How do you do, Caro. I hope you won't find this place too far from things. I will be writing quite a few social letters, answering condolences. That kind of thing. You type?"

101

"Oh, yes," the girl said with almost pathetic eagerness. "But I am also to do a little cleaning and dusting when the chambermaids aren't up here. And I can iron things and wash them for you. Help with your lovely hair. Maybe cook some meals when you don't want any—" She laughed nervously "—any gourmet cooking from the Spa. I'm really here to be—well—whatever you and Mr. Dulane need."

"Dugald," said Arthur, without emphasis.

The girl apologized and made the amendment. Kay was sure, by the girl's perfectly ordinary correction, that she had used the name in ignorance of any special meaning. Kay did not look at Arthur and she thought he ignored her during the few seconds that the name "Dulane" lingered on the air.

"You can hire someone to do that kind of work," Kay told the girl. "Don't worry about it. And there will be times when you will take your orders . . ." She had almost added ". . . from Arthur Dugald." It occured to her belatedly that in the event Arthur did turn out to be The Enemy, she wouldn't want him to be receiving a lot of gratuitous help from this girl so she amended lamely, ". . . take your orders for some very trivial things."

This time there was no question that Dugald understood Kay's amended statement, and he looked at her quickly. Caro Teague, however, assured her with that frantic nervousness she had exhibited before, "No, no! Whatever you say. It's absolutely vital that I hold a job. I mean—I must be working. Otherwise, I won't be kept in the . . . the employment file at the Cove."

"Good," Kay said. "Come along upstairs, Caro, and we'll see about your sleeping facilities. Arthur is going to be staying down here in this room. And there is an extra bedroom upstairs. Did you bring your things?"

The girl waved a hand at her small canvas airline bag and picked it up before Arthur could do so. She seemed so grateful to work for Kay that the latter found it embarrassing. They went up the circular steps together while Arthur Dugald remained below. He went over to the west end of the room. Kay wondered if he was still examining the cellar lock, or remembering the idiotic conversation they had had about the television set.

Caro Teague looked around the bed-sitting room, admiringly. "I love it. I had no idea she has it so good up here." She gave an uneasy giggle. "Or I'd have visited her earlier. How many bedrooms are up here?"

"Only two that we can find. Miss Teague—Caro—would you mind very much sleeping in that room beyond the bathroom?"

Bewildered, the girl walked over to the bathroom and opened the door into the dark bedroom against the mountainside. She called back, "I don't understand, Mrs. Aronson. If I sleep here and you there, and Mr. Dul—Mr. Dugald downstairs, where does Edna Schallert sleep?"

Kay looked at her, wondering if she had misunderstood the girl.

"Miss Schallert doesn't live here any more. She left in order to move into the Spa before my husband came here last month. Didn't she tell you she had moved?"

"But she couldn't! Edna signed a contract to remain here."

"A lease, you mean. Yes, I know. But my husband owned this chalet. She was only here in our absence."

Caro Teague peered nearsighedly into the dark bedroom, then at the bathroom, raising her voice in an uncharacteristic fashion as she protested. "Not a lease. You don't understand. Edna couldn't just pack up and move out of the Cove. She owed too much. The first one. A fellow named Gene Standish. And then, later, there was Buddy Hemplemeier. You see she owes for them."

"Owes for them! You mean they were gigolos?" Kay asked in confusion. Everyone seemed to be crazy here except herself.

"Not gigolos. No. Buddy was especially rich. But Edna made an agreement. And she signed. I know. She told me so."

When the girl came into the big, comfortable bed-sitting room again, Kay told her reasonably, "I think we must allow for the likelihood that Miss Schallert had enough of this place so when my husband came to take over the chalet, she left the Cove."

Kay had never seen a woman wring her hands but Caro Teague was doing just that, pulling at her fingers and massaging the thin flesh frantically in her excitement. "She couldn't! She was in the other file. I told her that. I warned her." She looked up, saw Kay staring at her with sympathy, but with shock too, and she sniffed and quickly brought herself under control. "I didn't mean to act so silly. Don't tell anyone. Please. I need this job so much. And it'll never happen again. I promise you."

She was so eager and so friendly Kay found it impossible not to like her. The girl obviously had problems. The least Kay could do was to help her out in this small way.

EIGHT

The chalet appeared surprisingly more cheerful with the addition of another woman. Kay liked to talk as well as most females, and since she suspected both the attractive men with whom she was involved at Lucifer Cove, she welcomed a companion as friendly and probably innocent as Caro Teague. Surely, no one who might be involved in a plot against Leo Aronson would be so terrified of losing her job!

On thinking it over during the afternoon, however, it occurred to Kay that innocent Carolyn Teague might have a very good reason for clinging to the job here at the chalet. If she had been sent by Leo's murderers to spy on Leo's widow. The only consolation Kay had after this chilling idea hit her was in the conduct of the girl herself.

Caro was just as nervous, just as eager after the two women had been together for several hours, putting Kay's things away, discussing the rapid change in hemlines, and European cities that they agreed or disagreed about.

"We performed in loads of places," Caro

bubbled on enthusiastically. "It was kind of confusing sometimes. We moved about so much I'd wake up thinking, 'Here we are in Genoa' when we had already moved on to Milan or Verona or Venice or some such place."

"You were an actress? That must be fascinating. I used to want to be a movie star."

They laughed together, in understanding. But Caro corrected her. "I was a dancer, actually. Ricardo Shahnaz' partner. We were called Ricardo and Caro. You didn't . . ." Her voice held a kind of poignance that touched Kay. "You didn't happen to see us—ever?"

Kay reluctantly shook her head.

Caro added, "We were very good."

Kay said, "I know you must have been, and I imagine you were very popular, a girl with your looks. What happened? I don't mean to be prying, but from the way you move, so slowly and gracefully, you are a born dancer."

"Slowly and gracefully! That's rather funny. I walk that way because I'm lame. I can hide the lameness better."

Kay felt guilty and obtrusive. "I beg your pardon. And that is why you quit, of course."

"But you see, it was so unfair! I mean, there was no reason why Ricardo should have been—what's the word?—ostracized just because of a little quarrel. Anyway, I broke my leg and ankle. The ankle healed. The patella, my knee, was never right afterward. It was my fault that I fell. I was just clumsy. He didn't push me, the way they said. He just let me go too soon. But that, on top of his reputation with—well, women were crazy about him—just ruined him. They exaggerated everything horribly. He couldn't get a job anywhere. Not the kind he wanted. One day he got an offer to come to this place. I was still in the hospital but they told him to bring a girl. So instead of getting a girl that wasn't crippled, he got me."

Kay found the girl's own innocence in the one-sided love affair more poignant than the sordid story itself. "And your partner, this Ricardo, works here at the Cove?"

The girl raised her head. The tears still sparkled in her eyes but her young face looked old with bitterness and hate.

"No! He died here last spring. That dreadful priestess woman, Nadine Janos, she put a hex on him and killed him. Dr. Rossiter at the Cove here said it was a heart attack. Ricardo died while he was swimming in the Sea-Green pool. But I know better. Nadine got her precious Lord Satan to kill him."

Kay's natural sympathy for the masochistic Caro was slightly diluted by her interest in these confessions. Whatever Caro's lover had done to these people at Lucifer Cove, there seemed to be faint indications that the unsavory Ricardo Shahnaz was murdered. Whatever was done, it had been clever to shift the blame onto the priestess. One could hardly arrest Nadine for praying the man to death.

Kay remarked aloud, but more or less to herself, "It's more than likely. Look at all the people who have died here."

"Careful," said Arthur Dugald who set a tray with a decanter and sherry glasses on the table between the two women.

Kay looked at him suspiciously but he repeated before she could say anything, "Careful, please. I seem to have spilled a few drops of sherry." But in spite of his bland look, she knew perfectly well he had been warning her.

"Too many die here. Too many," Caro murmured. "Oh, sherry. Thank you. I've been so nervous lately. And cocktails are no good. They give me a headache. But sherry relaxes me. Christie and I have a glass of sherry every afternoon that she's free."

"Christie?" It was Kay who asked the question, but she was very much aware of Arthur's sudden attention.

"Yes. Mr. Meridon's mistress. Christine Deeth. She has been very good to me, especially since Ricardo was—since Ricardo died," she amended. "It was Edna Schallert who persuaded Christie to come here a year ago after Christie had been very unhappy. Divorced and all. We all suspect down at the Cove that Mr. Meridon persuaded Edna to get Christie here. He had his eye on her for a long time."

Kay felt a small pinch of disappointment and realized, after some close self-examination, that she wanted to believe Marc Meridon was free of such ties as this one with Mrs. Deeth. There was nothing personal in her wish, surely. No desire that the mysterious and attractive owner of the Spa should look at Kay Aronson in that special way. It was an insult to all the close relationship, the good years with Leo. Yet there was a definite attraction about Mark Meridon that affected other women as it affected Kay.

If Meridon was actually involved in some way

with Leo's death, and if he suspected the true reason for Kay's arrival at the Cove, then he might have good and selfish reasons for trying to charm Kay. *Trying* to charm her? If so, he had succeeded all too well!

While Kay was thinking this over, she was surprised to find that Arthur Dugald had taken over the interrogation.

"Miss Teague, you mention the Schallert lady. Did you know her well?" The girl looked blank and he explained, "Were you in her confidence?"

Kay glanced at Caro and then, puzzled by the bitterness and aging hate in the girl's face, watched as Caro shrugged and answered, "You don't have to be in anybody's confidence to know people here. I mean, there is a kind of bond among us after we sign up."

"The glass is very small. Another sherry?"

Much intrigued by Arthur Dugald's play-acting—he was now performing "The Faithful Retainer"—Kay watched him but listened to the girl's half-confession and her curious reticence which must come from fear, since her hatred of Lucifer Cove was very evident.

Dugald's quiet voice pursued the truth. "And of course you signed. What else could you do?"

"That's right." Caro slapped the tabletop with the flat of her hand. "That's *right!* What else? Besides, Ricardo told me we must, or else we'd be thrown out. And the pickings were too good here; so we signed. I thought ..."

"Yes?"

"I don't know what I thought," Caro contradicted herself quickly. "Ricardo wanted it; so we did it."

Kay was so busy watching the girl and wondering, she was startled to see Dugald raise his head, look toward the living room's north windows. The room had been pleasantly glowing under the light from the two lamps, one near the low, beaten, bronze Egyptian table where they were having their cocktails, the other lamp across the room, on top of what Kay thought of as the haunted television set. There was a coziness about the curious round room that was a complete turnabout from the gloomy, depressing dark of the room by daylight.

"What is it, Arthur?" Kay asked, suddenly tense.

"The path out there seems remarkably busy, considering that it's scarcely dinnertime."

"They're out there, all right," Caro put in quickly, waving her sherry glass.

Arthur had started across the room to the windows that overlooked the trail. Kay asked him, "What is it? Are they coming here?" So many eerie things had happened since her arrival that morning, she should have been prepared for anything.

Caro reached out and touched her. "Don't worry. So long as you don't go there, you don't have to worry about that creature."

Arthur Dugald was at the window now, looking out. "I take it they are clients from the Cove on their way to Miss Janos' temple. Why are they passing this house?"

"There is another way up here from the village. Over to your left, among the trees. But it's awfully steep. Most of the devil worshippers come up the regular trail. That's about half mile east of us. You probably used it today."

Kay got up and went over to the window beside Dugald.

"What do you suppose they do at that temple?"

"The usual Satanic rites, I imagine. Simply a reversal of Christian rites. They are not very inventive, from what I've read."

She glanced at Caro. Across the room the girl was staring into her little gold-banded glass. Kay murmured, "Do you think the place is as dangerous as she says?"

"I doubt if the great Ricardo was destroyed by prayer. Even Satanic prayer."

"You think it was murder?"

Caro looked over at them, her large hazel eyes wide. "Someone's been murdered?" She started to get up in a great hurry but Kay motioned her to disregard their discussion.

"Nothing like that. We were just talking about the mental power this Satanic priestess may have."

"But it isn't that at all. She simply says things—suggests them—and they happen."

"The power of suggestion?" Dugald asked blandly.

"Sort of. She gets her orders, maybe." They both looked at her. She avoided their eyes, gazed down at her glass and twirled it between her fingers while Kay saw that Dugald was much more interested in Caro's artless little confidences than his position warranted. Unless, of course, there was one of two explanations: Either he shared Kay's own desire to learn the truth about Leo Aronson's death, or he wanted to find out all the girl knew for some more sinister reason. If he was actually some sinister creature who had been involved in the murder of a labor leader, then he might have his own reasons for pumping Caro Teague. She wished she could trust him. As a matter of fact, Kay wished she could trust anyone, including Marc Meridon and Caro herself.

Dugald asked Caro a few more questions but got nowhere and suddenly broke off to suggest that they look into the dinner situation. Kay agreed enthusiastically, having eaten little during the day, and they adjourned to the kitchen to investigate the situation.

While Kay and Dugald got down a number of possible edible combinations, Caro shivered and huddled into the unattractive cardigan sweater and skirt she was wearing. Kay, looking down at her from a white-enameled step stool, suggested to Dugald, "I think Miss Teague is coming down with pneumonia. It's that accursed fog outside."

She half-expected Arthur to ignore the hint. He was not, after all, a bond-servant, nor was he likely to know where every gas-heater in the place was located, if, indeed, there were any. But he vanished into the living room while Caro, with apologies for having been remiss in her duties, took his place, asking hopefully, "Could we all make do with canned corned beef hash with egg on top?"

Recalling suddenly, and vividly, the many camping trips on which she and Leo had shared such makeshift and delicious meals, Kay agreed that nothing could be better for a gloomy night with clammy cold everywhere, but added with a

113

laugh, "I'd like to know how many months the eggs have been here."

"Oh, not long, I shouldn't think. Miss Schallert liked fresh eggs for breakfast; so that wouldn't be longer than—maybe—sixteen days ago."

Kay wrinkled her nose but decided Caro was right. Caro got out the eggs from the refrigerator and set a percolator with coffee going. Both women were going into pleasant minor ecstasies over the odor of perking coffee when Kay began to sniff, and glanced around.

"A fire! Bless the man! He's started a fire in there."

She and Caro dashed into the living room and huddled before the great, crackling fire.

"Heavenly!" Kay exclaimed, rubbing her hands and holding them, palms out, to the fire. But she found Caro's conduct a little odd. The girl got so close to the grate she had to slap out sparks from her skirt. Then, she stared at the flames in the most curious way, with a drawn, haggard look on her face that aged her.

"Caro, what are you thinking?" Kay asked in spite of the feeling that she was prying into matters which were none of her business.

Starting, as if interrupted in deep thought, the girl murmured, "About Ricardo, in hell."

That jarred Kay. "But Caro, I thought you loved him. How could you possibly think he would wind up in hell? Assuming there is one." The girl made no reply and Kay looked helplessly across the room at Arthur Dugald who was bringing a second big cubed floor cushion to join the first before the fire. It did not help Kay's mood to note the extraordinary intensity of his interest in the girl. Not that there appeared to be anything romantic, any softness. Maybe it wasn't in Dugald's nature. He waited for the girl to answer Kay but nothing happened.

Kay sat down for a minute or two, suggesting that the girl do likewise. Caro blindly found the cube cushion, seated herself and said suddenly, "I haven't done this for months. Ricardo used to like it. He said Miss Schallert arranged to have wood piled up for practically the whole winter behind the chalet."

Kay remembered suddenly, "Arthur, is that where you got these logs under the kindling?"

"No. These were in that cord of wood in the cellar at the foot of the steps."

"Cellar?" Caro cried. "I didn't know this place had a cellar. I don't believe Edna knew either."

Kay said uneasily, "You did go down there, and alone! You know I wanted to see what it was all about."

But Dugald was smooth, calm as a perfect butler. "I found it dusty, the steps quite steep for a woman. The cellar itself would bore you, I'm sure, Mrs. Aronson. I can make a report to you about the rest of the cellar."

"We'll see about it tomorrow. I'm not about to go exploring tonight, I promise you that," Kay laughed, a little self-consciously, hoping to get everyone into a mood less funereal. She was beginning to discover that her first burning thirst for revenge after the loss of her husband, a thirst that had kept her going, kept her from crying, now degenerated into a horrible, pervasive suspicion of everyone. It was so unlike the ever-positive moods of Leo himself that she felt she had to, at least, raise the spirits of those present, suspicious characters or not. For one thing, it was what Leo himself would have done.

"Well, mysterious cellar or whatever, we've got to eat. I was a pretty fair country cook when my husband and I went camping up in the Blue Ridge. Shall we have our dinner on trays in front of the fire?"

She was pleased out of all proportion at Dugald's enthusiasm for the idea. Caro Teague, aroused from her mood, hurried after Kay to help her. Dugald set up a little round table with an Egyptian mosaic pattern before the fireplace and moved up another big cushion.

It was a highly successful dinner. There was a surprising amount of joking and laughter. Kay found an entirely new Arthur Dugald. Either he had taken a fancy to the haggard but pretty Caro Teague, or he was trying to learn something from the girl and set out to charm her into telling him anything she might know. There were moments when he looked over her head at Kay, significantly, and she wondered if he was trying to tell her something. But nothing the girl said made too much sense, except that she was awfully scared and could hardly open her mouth about the workings of Lucifer Cove without shivering and sinking into a gloomy apathy.

Kay was surprised at how pleasantly sleepy she was at the end of the evening. No barbiturates tonight. Not even time for lying in bed thinking about the long life ahead without the dear companionship of Leo Aronson.

Sending Caro up to the back bedroom when she began to nod and yawn, Kay walked out on the step and stared along the trail, trying to make out the doings in the white temple of Satan. When Dugald sauntered out behind her, she remarked,

"Looks harmless in the fog, doesn't it?"

"It probably is. It's that woman—that Janos creature—who plants ideas in people's minds, and they go out and believe what she tells them. Like voodoo."

"Possibly."

She hardly knew how to take that. It must be his weird sense of humor.

"You know what orgies, what rottenness must go on there. It's odd . . ." She broke off.

"What is odd, Kay? What are you thinking?"

Frowning, she tried to think back through all the time with Leo, all the confidences exchanged. Most of his past history; all of hers. "He never mentioned this place. He never mentioned that rotten, obscene temple."

"Mr. Aronson?"

"Did he mention it to you?"

"Never. But I still say his nightmares were the key to it."

She almost whispered because she felt, in this ghostly night, that anyone could be listening, "To his death?"

"To his murder."

"Then you *do* believe it! Is that really why you wanted to come here? To find out who gave the order and who killed him?"

He glanced over his shoulder, back into the big, round living room where the fire still smouldered, casting a cheerful, flickering light over the scene.

"I am more interested in Mr. Aronson than in

117

his killers. He presented himself to his killers, I believe. That is what puzzles me. As I see it, he didn't want to come here. That explains his dreams, I suspect. *So why did he come to the Cove?* That seems to me much more important than the individual enemies he may have had."

Kay reminded him quickly, "But he left. He tried to get away from here, and they stopped him. Somehow."

A titter of laughter cut eerily through the fog and Kay jumped. "What the devil was that?"

Arthur went quickly down the steps. He dissolved in the fog so fast she was impressed. He was always surprising her. She called, "What is it?"

For a minute or two she had the nasty, chilling sensation that he had vanished forever, like Leo.

"Arthur? Where are you?"

The whole landscape was shrouded in silence. Then, just as she was getting ready to rush down into that shroud of fog, Dugald emerged slowly, looking around in both directions.

"A night bird of some kind. I imagine that coven will be breaking up soon at the temple, so it might be best to get inside now."

"I'm certainly not afraid of them!" she insisted firmly.

"I wasn't thinking of fear. I was thinking of the drugs these covens go in for. "Opening up the mind" I think they call it."

She turned and hurried into the house. "You are right. I want no part of that scene."

They said good night at the foot of the circular steps.

"Tomorrow," she announced, "I may look into

that temple business. See what that woman and her coven are up to. Don't you think there is something to that?"

"There may be, but I would be failing Mr. Aronson if I let you wander into that snake pit alone. We'll see how it can be handled."

"We might put on an act. Pretend to be interested in the villainous devil worship."

"Excellent." He put his hand out and quite simply, without suspicion or thought, she put her hand into his. "I promise you, we will find out what happened to Mr. Aronson. Good night."

Her head was whirling when she went up to the bed-sitting room. She could have sworn in those moments that Arthur Dugald was completely trustworthy. But was Adam Dulane a man to trust? She decided tomorrow she would phone to Detroit to check on that mysterious Dulane.

Meanwhile, with the Indian blankets, serapes and rugs everywhere, the bed-sitting room looked cozy and inviting. The heat from the fireplace had traveled up the circular steps remarkably well and in spite of the fog outside the atmosphere inside was anything but ominous and depressing. As Kay finished undressing for her shower and bed, she wrapped herself in a comfortable velvour robe and knocked on the bathroom door that opened into Caro Teague's bedroom.

The girl opened the door, looking astonishingly glamorous and beautiful. She wore a green nylon chiffon nightgown and peignoir which brought out the heretofore subdued loveliness of her pale red hair. She had been brushing that hair until it framed her face and fell in a cascade to her shoulders, slightly unruly, with a natural curl, and a look Kay felt would be extremely sensuous to a man, even a man of great self-control like Arthur Dugald. Kay would not have been human and female if she hadn't been jealous of that transformation. But she managed to subdue the unworthy emotion and complimented the girl instead.

"My dear Caro, why do you hide your looks? I'm sure if you look like that all the time you will break every heart at the Cove, and you can certainly find someone—not to take your friend Ricardo's place exactly—but to be, forgive me, a better risk."

"It was Ricardo who taught me to look like this," the girl said simply.

Kay was heartily sick of that dubious paragon, Ricardo Shahnaz, but she managed not to show her dislike for Caro's favorite subject.

"Do you find your bedroom reasonably comfortable?"

Caro held the door open for Kay to look in. By lamplight the room did a complete about-face from the gloomy tomb it resembled by daylight.

"It's very nice. I have a small room at the Spa but the Spa is more elegant. Less comfortable and homelike than Miss Schallert's place here. That is to say, Mr. Aronson's place."

"Good. Just let me know tomorrow if you want anything changed. Good night, now."

The girl said good night and went back inside. Kay wondered if Caro was unaware of her predecessors in that bed. But as long as the girl liked the room, why go into all its "haunted" qualities?

Kay showered and then, in the bright sitting

room, brushed her own hair until it sparkled and glistened to her satisfaction. She heard nothing in the living room below and, just before getting into bed, she went over to the metal steps and looked down, listening. Dugald must have gone instantly to sleep. She envied him the ability. As she watched down that corkscrew of metallic steps, she saw an occasional flickering shadow from the fireplace, and heard several sharp cracks as a burnt log fell into the bed of flames. However, this noise apparently did not disturb Dugald. There was no other sound in the shadowed room at the foot of the steps.

Kay went over to the windows, began to close the drapes. Arthur had been right. The Coven, a quarter of a mile along the mountainside toward the main trail, had broken up and some of Nadine Janos' acolytes must be hurrying down the trail. Through the fog she made out weird, indefinite black forms. They must be still wearing the black penitent robes and peaked hoods which were the temple uniform.

Several temple strays were on their way past the chalet, directly below Kay's windows. They certainly made a sinister appearance, moving along like the very essence of deadly menace, faces and hands hidden. Eyes flashing through two holes in a black hood, the foremost devil-worshipper gazed up at the chalet's front, almost as if the creature guessed that Kay was there behind the edge of the drape, watching him. She stepped back hurriedly. When the black figure and two following had passed, she closed the drapes and went to bed.

But the drapes were not quite closed. As she

lay in the comfort of the wide bed with its superb mattress and stiff, cool sheets, the fog pushed in like little fingers, up and down the slit of light where the drapes did not overlap.

In spite of this Kay got to sleep in a surprisingly short time.

She was completely comfortable, even in her dreams. So much so that for several hours the odd little sounds of an unfamiliar house at night did not disturb her.

But at 2:10 A.M., according to the illuminated hands of her bedside clock, there was a light, though definite series of noises, whose origin she couldn't place at once in her half-sleep. Then she sat up abruptly, grateful for the tell-tale streak of foggy light from the window. She had remembered where she heard that sound earlier in the evening, that peculiar, muffled metallic sound of footsteps on the circular steps.

NINE

Silently, she got out of bed and slipped barefoot across the room over the bright red, white and black Indian rug to the wrought-iron top rail of the steps. The faint light that her eyes had become accustomed to showed her no one was now on the steps. She couldn't see beyond and below the steps.

She looked around her own room. The bathroom door was ajar. She was sure she had closed it earlier in the night. A suspicion suddenly occurred to her. She went to the bathroom, fumbled for the old-fashioned knob of the door into the back bedroom. The first thing she noticed was that the drapes to one window had been opened, giving some light to the room. It seemed odd, but not impossible that Caro Teague preferred to sleep in a room which was so light. There was a lucid quality about the fog at that window.

Kay stood in the doorway long enough to become accustomed to that curious light emanating from the fog which crowded in at the window. There was no one in the bed. The entire room was empty. No Caro Teague here, hiding in a corner, or among the bedclothes, or in a closet. There was a closet. Kay opened the door, saw that it was empty, and leaving the closet door open hurried out to the circular steps.

"What in the world is she up to?"

It infuriated Kay to think the girl must have sneaked out past her, through her own room and she had not heard a sound until too late. What was Caro Teague really after? Prying around, no doubt. Hoping to find out something about Kay and her mission here, to report to the owners of the Cove.

Kay stopped long enough to get a miniature flashlight from her handbag, step into quilted satin flats and put on her velour robe. She went silently down the steps. The padded satin slippers did not betray her. The living room, too, appeared to be deserted. She stood at the bottom of the circle steps to get her bearings. There was a certain degree of light cutting across the room from the kitchen. It enabled Kay to see that Arthur Dugald wasn't on his studio couch either.

Kay made her way carefully around the room. No question about it, Arthur was not here. The downstairs bathroom door was ajar. He was not in there.

She had circled the room with such care she did not run into anything in the semi-dark until she reached the big television console which looked perfectly blank and natural but reminded her of something so preposterous she hardly credited her own idea. She stepped back a few feet, knelt and without operating the light in the palm of her hand, she felt along the floor until she found the lock on the cellar door. Preposterous or not, the lock and hasp were separated, the cellar door was unlocked.

Kay hesitated, looked around and then, finding no one behind her, neither Arthur nor Caro, nor one of the weird black penitents from the devil's temple, she raised the door which proved to be scarcely more than a wooden lid with a wooden lid's creaking noises when she opened it. She peered down the steep flight of steps, wondering where the light came from; for the cellar, while in shadows, was unquestionably illuminated from a distance.

Were they both down there? And if so, were they in this business together, ganging up on her for some reason?

She had a very nasty notion of a joke, to lock the cellar door. But she restrained herself and left the trap door open, stuffed two couch cushions in around it, and cinched its position by jamming the poker into the big hinges. Then she listened. Still no sound below. She went over to the hutch across the room and reached into a drawer, getting out the surprisingly heavy, if somewhat unreliable, thirty-two automatic she had bought after Leo's death. She had read too many novels in her day to allow herself to be trapped, knocked on the head and murdered. She held it up to the light between the drapes, checked the cartridge clip. It was fully loaded.

With her right hand on the automatic in the pocket of her robe and the miniature flashlight in her left hand, she went slowly, with infinite care, down the steps. Whatever footprints Arthur Dugald had seen early in the day were blotted out now by other footprints. At least two sets. The man's prints were undoubtedly Arthur's. Early in the evening he had gone down to get wood for the fire. But there was a second set of woman's prints. Small soles and a tiny stab of a heel mark. Caro Teague's?

There was a certain degree of light on the steps. Its source appeared to be deep in the further recesses of the cellar. She glanced at the wood stacked beside the steps. The pile was smaller, obviously, than it had been early in the day. Kay stopped and listened, heard nothing. But when she took several steps in the opposite direction, into what appeared to be a large annex to the little cellar, she thought she made out a distant sound, magnified by these walls. Frightening walls, of dirt and shale and stone.

What *was* that sound? Inhuman, somehow. Not a groan or a cry. Simply a sound.

There was no end to this curious cellar. She decided it was no longer a cellar when the squarish beginnings began to squeeze off into something like a tunnel. The dim light came from there. What had Arthur said about other caves just over the eastern range of the valley? It began to look as if this cellar exploration was a job for a speleologist, certainly not for a woman with no karate talents and no head for depths.

She heard the noise again, twisted and turned and blurred by the walls. Incredible! It now began to suggest an animal's howl.

"Good God! Howling wolves lying in wait under my own house? I must be dreaming."

All the same, she stopped where she was, considered the hour, what she was doing here, and

126

whether she was capable of hitting anything with the Beretta, even if she fired. She was now obviously in the tunnel or the beginning of a series of low-roofed caves which snaked downward in a kind of step fashion. She couldn't be sure where the cellar mysteriously changed into the caves. It had simply narrowed at its northern end. Since the caves led down and north it seemed clear they would wind up below in the valley. Very likely in the village itself.

She began to retreat, moving backward, but the scene ahead was now more illuminated. She had been close to something, someone with a light, when she gave up. She listened. Another sound reached her. Faintly. Water dripping. It did not surprise her. In caves like this there was sure to be seepage, from underground springs, or possibly even salt water. They were not far from the ocean. A few yards around the next turn would answer some of the riddles. The light that was beginning to increase in volume was certainly not held by an animal, even that ferocious liver-colored hound!

The sounds were audible enough for her to identify them: the mingled sobbing and mumbling of someone in the last stages of unspeakable terror. She almost fell over a woman's foot in a torn nylon stocking. Then the leg. An older woman. The leg was bony, with a tiny network of varicose veins almost masked by the dark color of the flesh. Her suit skirt and jacket were badly ripped.

A big flashlight startled Kay still more by rolling toward her on the damp surface of the cave. She saw that the woman's face and upper trunk were concealed by the kneeling body of Caro Teague who was rocking back and forth, moaning, her fingers tight-locked together. Before Kay spoke she was sure the sprawled, motionless body was that of the missing Edna Schallert.

"Caro, is she dead? Let me see."

The girl was in shock and did not seem to hear her. She moved the girl gently to one side and glanced at the dead woman's face, then looked away quickly. She had a good stomach for most things but the woman had obviously been dead for many days, probably since before Leo's death. Kay felt a nasty unsteadiness in her stomach, like wings beating. She was perilously close to being sick.

With furious determination she swallowed several times until the feeling went away. There was still the odor, a peculiar, nauseously sweet odor. She and Caro could not stay here.

"Come. We must get help . . ."

The girl still stared glassily at the dead woman and it was necessary to take her by the shoulders and forcibly pull her away.

"Caro! Stop that! Do you hear me?"

The hideous keening went on, punctuated by gulps for breath, but the girl let herself be drawn away and onto her feet unsteadily. Kay supported her with some difficulty while looking around the area. The roof of the cavelike tunnel was rocky and water seeped out in droplets onto her head, joining the tiny finger-width stream running along the west wall of the tunnel. Already, Kay's velour robe was soggy, mud-crusted around her bare ankles. The touch made her shiver.

She had a strong inclination to run as fast as

she could, back the way she had come. But the condition of the dead woman's clothing baffled her. All those slits and tears, like the teeth or the claws of an animal that had worried the material. But the woman's flesh did not suggest a physical attack. Had she died and then been discovered in death by an animal? Or was it possible that the sight of the animal gave her a heart attack?

"Caro, did you see anything in here?"

The girl stared at her with glazed eyes. "Anything? I saw . . . her."

"No, no. An animal. Did you see an animal of any kind?" The girl shook her head vaguely. "Or hear one?"

She thought Caro Teague was paying no attention to her words, but when she left the girl long enough to pocket her own light and pick up the big flashlight Caro had brought, she surprised the girl peering nearsightedly down the dark recesses of the tunnel beyond. Kay's fingers closed around the Beretta that weighted her right pocket. She hoped she did not look as shaky as she felt.

"What do you see, Caro?"

"Nothing . . . I heard a kind of scuffling noise."

They listened, Caro clutching at Kay's arm in a way that made her terror contagious.

"Do you hear it, Mrs. Aronson? There. Scuffling. Scrabbling. Like . . ."

Kay wrapped her fingers carefully around the automatic, and took a few steps around a jutting series of rocks. Just beyond the circle of light there was something, unmistakably; like a tiny light burning, very near the rugged earth floor. When she made out a twin light and hurried on a few feet, she knew before her flashlight picked it out, that the lights were the eyes of a small animal. She had been braced for the terrors of the pale, liver-colored hound. When she saw the huge, round eyes of Kinkajou, the striped tabby cat, he looked quite as surprised as she was. She began to laugh. There was a note of hysteria in the sound, and the cat drew itself up into a bristling horseshoe of feline indignation.

Kay looked him over but could not touch him. He certainly had healed fast. Yesterday morning he had almost bled to death. Now, except for a handful of missing hair along his throat, he seemed quite cured. Unless, of course, this was a different cat.

Caro called to her in panic. "The light's going. Don't go any further, Mrs. Aronson! Don't leave me."

Kay left the cat to his own devices and retraced her steps to Caro and the body of the unfortunate Edna Schallert. During those few seconds it occurred to her that the cat might be responsible for the shredding of the dead woman's clothing. It was a particularly distasteful thought because the little cat had aroused her sympathy during its struggle with the great hound, but as she motioned Caro along the tunnel back to the main cellar, and looked back at the pathetic sprawled body of Edna Schallert, she still could not be sure. There must be rodents underground here, or gophers, or squirrels might have chewed at that cloth. But why hadn't they eaten the flesh?

She was so overwhelmed by this horror that she hurried Caro until they were both running.

Caro was a few steps ahead of her and when they reached the foot of the cellar steps Caro shrieked and stopped abruptly. Expecting some new monstrous apparition, Kay cried out as well, and was still badly shaken when she saw Arthur Dugald peering down at them from the trap door at the top of the steps.

"Good God! What are you two doing down there?" he wanted to know. "Do you realize what time it is?"

Kay said abruptly, "Never mind that. I'll tell you later. We've found Edna Schallert. That is to say, Miss Teague found her. Would you call the Spa and have them contact the police?"

"And doctors?" he asked, efficient as always, but she thought their discovery had jarred him this time.

"I'm afraid she's been dead quite a while."

"I'll see to it." He didn't waste time on questions, but helped Kay and Caro up the steps and then took the flashlight Kay offered him and went down into the cellar. Caro was shivering and obviously helpless, so Kay dragged a log over into the fireplace, stirred up the embers with the poker, and the two women sat down, stretching their hands out to the fire.

"Wasn't that odd?" Caro asked suddenly, her voice high-pitched and strange, coming out of the darkness of the big room.

"Yes. More than odd. It was grisly."

"I didn't mean about Edna Schallert. That's not odd. I mean—Mr. Dugald was fully dressed. Does he always go around fully dressed at three o'clock in the morning?"

Kay looked across the room at the couch where

131

Dugald had presumably slept. She wondered why she hadn't thought it odd an hour ago, but the couch had not been made up into a bed. Did Arthur ever sleep?

She said, "Well, I can't put it off. Arthur may be wandering around down there for hours. I'll have to make the call." She got up and went to the telephone.

Still staring into the fire, Caro murmured, "We shouldn't have left him alone."

Kay heard the night operator's sleepy voice at the Spa and started to speak, then covered the mouthpiece. "What do you mean? Do you think he is in danger?"

In an astonishingly hopeful voice, considering the circumstances, the girl suggested, "Maybe he killed Edna. Couldn't he have done it?"

"No, he couldn't! She has been dead for over a week, and Mr. Dugald didn't arrive here until yesterday morning with me. As a matter of fact," she went on angrily, "we don't even know anybody killed Miss Schallert. She may have wandered down there for some reason and just died. Hello? This is Mrs. Aronson at the chalet. We've found a dead woman."

"I suppose it could have happened that way," Caro said, still in that hopeful tone.

Kay nodded and related the facts briefly, but brief as she was, it puzzled her to discover how calmly her news was received by the female at the Spa. She set the phone back. The gesture was slow and deliberate, unlike her usual rapid movements.

"They are coming, and they are bringing a doctor."

132

She looked across the room, seeing the uncertain silhouette of the girl, but the scarlet light twisted and elongated Caro Teague's features until the pink-bronze hair, the haggard face and gaunt young body cast monstrous shadows against the brickwork above the fireplace.

Like something out of a devil's cauldron, she thought, and was amazed at her own sinister thought about this perfectly ordinary girl.

"Caro, why weren't they surprised at the Spa?"

Caro looked up slowly, as if from a deep sleep. "Did you say something, Mrs. Aronson?"

"No." Kay stood there motionless for what seemed to her an embarrassing time before she joined the girl at the fire. She appeared to be warming herself at the crackling flames but her curiosity and suspicions about the girl were growing with each minute they sat there in close proximity, like mutually trusting friends.

Was this, somehow, different only in its details, the way death had come to Leo Aronson? First the fear as in Caro Teague when she arrived at the chalet. Then there were the peculiar actions: in Caro, her middle-of-the-night venture into what should be a place of terror that cellar beneath the chalet. With Leo, the fear was in those nightmares, and then, like Caro Teague, the journey into that very terror.

"It must be getting toward dawn," Kay remarked presently and as the girl stared at her dully, "I wonder how the woman did die." She hoped to induce her companion to some betrayal of her knowledge, but Caro Teague, who had raised her head as if to answer, turned suddenly.

"They are coming." She appeared to be trembling but tried to cover her betrayal by getting up. "Shall I let them in, Mrs. Aronson?"

"Please."

But Kay saw Arthur Dugald coming up the cellar steps behind the girl, and when Caro had hurried across the room to the door, as if anxious to oblige Lucifer Cove's employees, Kay crossed behind her to the open trap door of the cellar.

"Do you know the details?" Dugald asked her in his quiet way, glancing at Caro who had opened the door to several figures dimly seen in the drifting fog of the porch.

Kay nodded. "I had a feeling they knew even before I called. What did you find?" She thought he looked a little pale, the faint network of lines around his eyes a trifle more pronounced, but otherwise, she felt the now-familiar reliance upon him. She marveled as always that he looked like a very ordinary man, considering how extraordinarily competent he was.

"She has been dead, at the very least, since Mr. Aronson left here."

"Murdered?"

"There are no signs that I can see. Of course, she may have been poisoned, though I can't imagine why." He was watching the three men who had entered with Caro across the room. His expression had tightened. She felt the significance of that and looked back over her shoulder.

"Good God!" she muttered to Dugald. "I expected Spa employees, along with Mr. Meridon. But those fellows look like motorcycle cops."

"They hardly look like visitors I'd welcome at

this hour. Shall I gird my loins for an encounter?"

"Please . . . And Arthur—" as he passed her, "—thank you."

She watched him approach the two men in black leather and white bubble-helmets that made them look all the more sinister. There was a mechanical precision about them, a total lack of human quality. "Zombies," she thought, smiling wryly at the absurd simile, but as Caro came to her she caught herself before saying it aloud. After all, she did not entirely trust Caro Teague, either.

"That's Dr. Rossiter," Caro explained. "Clive Rossiter. He has charge of the clinic and the rejuvenating halls of the Hot Springs. He won the Helsingford Prize for experiments on animal transplants several years ago. Youngest man ever to win it. But something went wrong, and he wound up here. Working to make flabby old men and women young again. He must hate it."

The black leather zombies, complete with high-gloss boots, clanked across the floor and past Kay toward the trap door to the cellar without a single question or even a greeting to her. It was as if they did not see her. Their faces were fleshy and florid, but their eyes had the opaque look of blue-ice, and she found herself drawing back from them in the most cowardly way.

Arthur startled her by appearing suddenly with a person perhaps no less terrifying than the leather zombies but with better manners. Caro Teague was right. The man in a white, belted smock such as surgeons must have worn before Kay Aronson's day, was younger than she imagined the Cove's resident physician and rejuvenator would be. His face was not unattractive, but the flesh was pulled tight over the bone structure, the eyes deep-set and very dark grey, with the cold passion of an intellectual fanatic, a dreamer of great deeds whose earthly connections had failed him.

"Dr. Clive Rossiter, Mrs. Aronson. I've explained about the finding of the body. We assume it is a woman named Edna Schallert. Seems to have been down there for some time."

"I assume the ladies who found the body are quite upset. Will they need anything?" Dr. Rossiter's accent was north-of-England, overlaid by a London education. In other circumstances she would have liked his voice, but at this time, judged by the company he kept, everything he did was frightening.

"We are perfectly all right, Doctor. Don't mind us."

A man of few words, the doctor went rapidly down the cellar steps after the leather pair with the bubble-helmets. Caro Teague had dropped down on the studio couch near the door and seemed to be in a stupor of fear. Kay, who had a strong inclination to burst into hysterics before retiring to a bed for twelve hours, found it absolutely essential that somebody make some hot tea. Arthur Dugald turned from watching the cellar steps to smile at Kay. The sight of his cheerfulness gave her a lift as she went into the dark kitchen.

She fumbled for the light switch while, behind her, Dugald reached over her head and snapped it on.

"What about reheating the coffee?"

She explained regretfully, "Then I'd never sleep," and set Edna Schallert's avocado-green enamel tea kettle on the electric burner. It seemed to her that she was excessively aware of Edna Schallert's influence here. She did not feel sad. She had never known the woman, after all. But she was aware of a peculiar guilt because she felt only horror at the discovery.

"Do you think this business has any connection with Leo?" she asked when the percolator had stopped perking and the tea kettle was beginning to steam.

Dugald was setting up a tray for the two women and started to say something but suddenly stopped. Kay was repeating her question when she too realized Caro Teague was standing in the kitchen doorway, resting her head tiredly against the door.

"What did you say about Mr. Aronson?" she asked in an exhausted voice.

Kay started to say something but Dugald cut her off with a sharp, almost rude interruption.

"Nothing, Miss Teague. Will you have cream or lemon? We've canned cream and plastic lemons."

The girl smiled, with pale, colorless lips. "Anything so long as it's hot. I feel as if I were freezing."

When the three of them were drinking in the little old-fashioned breakfast nook, Kay, who couldn't control herself any longer, raised the steaming coffee cup to her lips and over the rim, asked Caro pointedly,

"How on earth did you know Edna Schallert was in that tunnel? It was clever of you. I would never have guessed . . . about the tunnel, I mean. What made you go down there in the first place, and in your gown and robe, too, at that hour?"

Kay sensed the deep tension in Arthur Dugald, though he said nothing. Perhaps he was wondering when it would be his turn to do some explaining. Why hadn't he gone to bed last night? Why hadn't he undressed, made the couch into a bed? Where had he been when she went downstairs after Caro Teague?

I'll leave that for later, she promised herself.

Meanwhile, Caro Teague, still pale, had at least stopped shaking as she drank her tea. She said in a haunted voice, "I dozed off, but that room! I felt odd! I can't explain it." She gave an hysterical giggle. "I felt crowded. Isn't that silly?"

Kay and Arthur exchanged furtive glances. They were embarrassed to be caught at it by Caro, who perked up briefly.

"What is it about that room?" Neither of them could think of an answer to that and Caro added dreamily, "I thought of Edna. You see, I knew she must be dead. I warned her."

"How did you happen to warn her, Miss Teague?" Arthur asked quietly.

Caro's hazel eyes opened wide. "That was the easiest part. I was subbing for Miss Idwel over at the Hot Springs and I saw the change in her file."

"Her file. A physician's records?"

"Something like that. She said she was going to leave. I told her it was too late."

"Too late?" Kay repeated. "What was her illness?" But this only produced a surprised stare from Caro.

"I've no idea. But I'd heard rumors about the

cellar. Buddy Hemplemeier was talking about it once at the Spa. He was Miss Schallert's last boyfriend. Committed suicide about two months ago when he lost everything in some kind of Stock Market plunge. I was in that room where Buddy used to sleep, and suddenly I remembered his talk about Edna's expandable cellar."

"Expandable!"

"That's what he called it. And that's when I went looking for her tonight." She shuddered. "It was awful. I fell over her, and I heard something. A kind of growl."

"Growl! It was Kinkajou, the little cat," Kay protested.

But Caro shook her head. "That was after you came. Before the—the cat, I heard this other thing." She looked up suddenly and unexpectedly. "The people at Hot Springs call it the hound of death. But it's nothing to do with Kinkajou. It only shows up when ..."

"Every time there is a death?" Kay hoped neither the girl nor Dugald caught the sarcasm in that question.

"Sort of." Much subdued, Caro stared at her cup and murmured, "Maybe I could sleep here in the kitchen, on the seat here. With a couple of pillows and a blanket it shouldn't be too hard, or ..."

Facing the matter honestly, Kay remarked to Dugald, "If we find that room too much for us, we can't expect to palm it off on her."

But Dugald was only half listening to her.

"They are taking an extraordinary time about their removal of the woman's body."

No one said anything for a few minutes. Then

139

Arthur Dugald got up and walked into the living room. He revived the fire, went down the cellar steps, ostensibly to get more wood, but Kay wondered. When he came back up, Kay met him as he stepped into the room.

"We may as well not wait for them," he said. "They are gone, the body and all."

"Gone!"

Just as she was picturing enchantment, witchcraft, and simply a Houdini disappearance act, Dugald said with a calm she deeply suspected, "A very simple, explanation, no doubt. There is another end to that tunnel, obviously, and they took it."

Kay glanced quickly at Caro Teague, but the girl gave away nothing of her knowledge. She simply stared from the kitchen doorway, looking wan and ghostly in the pale dawn light.

"Yes, Arthur, but . . ."

He merely looked at her, waiting. She clutched her head.

"Nothing. This place is a living nightmare. I don't know what to believe any more."

TEN

It was already dawn when Kay went up to the bedsitting room, changed her mud-crusted robe for a bright chiffon caftan, and lay down on the unmade bed, so nervous, her mind so full of the night's terrors, she was sure she would not sleep again for weeks. Some time during these minutes she fell asleep and didn't wake up until the day was well along. She blinked, yawned, and glanced around the cheerful room sleepily.

Realization of the night's events came belatedly, and she sat straight up on the bed, wondering at the silence everywhere. Was the whole house asleep, or, at any event, resting? Her head ached when she moved quickly.

"Not surprising," she thought. "I fought enough horrors in my dreams to give me worse than a headache." She sat there rubbing the back of her neck, yawning, and frowning at the effort it took to recall those garbled horrors.

. . . A wild, tail-lashing dragon spouting smoke, with a mouth wide enough to engulf me . . .

Well, that would be suggested by the fog and that weird cavern and tunnels which apparently honey-combed the mountain and valley! The memory didn't lift her headache. But there had been other troubling snatches of nightmares that she found less easy to explain. For one thing, she was abominably thirsty.

"That's odd! What the devil did I drink last night?"

She took one of the friendly, exactly right pillows and pressed its deliciously starched case against her forehead. The cool comfort of that touch soon sharpened her faculties.

"I dreamed of a man hovering over my bed. What was there about him that aroused my fear?"

A cloud of white before her eyes. . . . Probably the fog. But it had been close. Much closer than those windows across the room. Thirsty again, she reached for the pewter carafe on the miniature bronze tray-top of the bedstand. Any water carafe beside her bed was always barely within a long reach, ever since she had once overturned a steel carafe full of ice into bed between her first husband and herself. She had been accused of using the ice cubes as a hint to remove himself from her life. She often thought afterward that, subconsciously, she may have intended precisely what he suspected. He had been a very expensive investment.

But after that first disastrous marriage, she had been particularly careful to leave the ice water carafe barely at her fingertips. Curiously enough the pewter pitcher she held in her hands now was on the near side of the saucer-shaped bronze tabaret; much too near her hand if she reached out in the night.

The glass was beside the carafe. She set down the carafe and tapped her nails against the glass thoughtfully, recalling vague, disjointed details of those curious nightmares last night. Most vivid, the image of the white-clad man standing beside her bed...

Dr. Clive Rossiter? And if so, had he assistance in returning to the inside of the chalet? For example, Arthur, or Caro, or both?

She sniffed at the glass. However, almost anything might have been in it and she wouldn't have known one poison or one barbiturate from another. It certainly would explain her long sleep and her headache. But why?

She got up silently, went to the bathroom and drank a glass of tepid water, listening as she did so, but there were no betraying sounds from the big room below the circle steps. Remembering how easy it would be—and doubtless had been—to reach her through that unprotected flight of steps, she was almost ready to move down to the Spa. At least, there must be a few locked rooms among those sensuous and glorious suites Marc Meridon operated.

She laughed without making a sound. It might turn out that mysterious Marc Meridon, the Spa's owner, whom she had suspected even before she met him, was the only trustworthy person at Lucifer Cove. After all, he had saved her life. Well, nearly ... She might not have drowned in that sea-green pool, but she was mighty uncomfortable before Marc fished her out.

She looked over the wrought-iron rail, went

down a few steps and looked over the room below. The fire had gone out. Only one person was in the living room. Caro Teague, still in her filmy nylon, was curled up asleep on the couch under the windows with her coat thrown over her. There was no sign of Arthur Dugald.

"Maybe he's like Dracula. He doesn't sleep at night," she thought wryly.

Belatedly, she recalled the dark back bedroom against the mountainside, hurried through the bathroom again, and looked into the room. No one was there, but the bed was tumbled as if someone had been lying on the old, hand-embroidered coverlet. She examined the room, noting that when the drapes were opened there was an unexpectedly full and cheerful light pouring in across the chamber.

Nothing there. "I never did see a ghost in broad daylight," she told herself, finding a kind of gallows' humor in the entire idea of a room haunted by the memories of Edna Schallert's unfortunate boyfriends.

A few minutes later she found nothing suspicious in the front of the chalet either. She opened the window. The trail was empty. A watery sun shown upon the dry rooks, shale and dust. Further along, toward the Devil's Temple, it shown with particular brightness upon a man and woman whose presence interested Kay greatly.

Nadine Janos was walking in another of her startling black and white outfits, which turned out to be pajamas with a silky sheen. She was arguing with the tall, husky man with a map of Ireland on his face, a good deal of Irish temper in his clenched fists. He seemed to be the man she had caught a glimpse of inside the temple the day she arrived. He had smiled then and looked friendly enough, but it was clear that a battle royal was in progress.

Nadine said something, hauled off and slapped him, whereupon the big Irishman shouted loudly enough to reach Kay at the window: "I'll go no further with it, and be damned to you! You've used your wiles before and made fancy promises and all come to nothing. Your tongue wags at both ends and both are liars, is what they are!"

"Go on, then," the priestess screamed. "Take the shale path. It nearly did for that idiot preacher girl last month. Let it do the same for you then!"

In spite of the Irishman's temper and determination, Kay suspected he didn't really want to leave the devilish hellion. She was temporarily diverted by their quarrel. She excused herself for eavesdropping by telling herself the quarrel took her thoughts off the grim business at hand. And besides, she might learn something to her own advantage.

"Don't you be wishing me gone like the preacher girl. I'll not be running away. But I'll tell you this, Princess, it was me that helped her to get away. Me and old Edna. So you may put that in your pipe and smoke it."

To Kay's surprise Nadine Janos burst into laughter and pulled at the big Irishman's sleeve.

"What an anticlimax! 'Put it in your pipe.' Oh, Irish, don't be such a damned high-minded Mick. Come along. Forget it. I'll give you another cliche. 'You can't fight City Hall.'"

And after all their fighting, the Irishman gave

up and returned with her, and the two of them passed close under Kay's window, although the Irishman seemed to be tempting fate in the shape of another quarrel.

"Anyway, I stick to it. He was up here spying, and if it wasn't him doin' the spying, who'll it be? We'll be after finding ourselves in the wrong file."

It was a very odd conversation. Kay leaned back against the wall between the windows and tried to recall every word. She was sure there were clues in the conversation. Several clues. But she didn't understand any of them. She gave up playing detective for the moment. It only made her head ache. Instead, she ran a hot bath, massaged with her favorite perfumed bath oil, and dressed for the hazy, pre-spring morning at Lucifer Cove. She wasn't quite sure, off the top of her consciousness, what she intended to do, or above all, if there was anyone in this valley that she could trust. She would simply have to play it by ear.

Beneath the outward denials, though, there was a nagging hope that she would run into Marc Meridon, more or less "by accident" and find reason to trust him, if all the others failed her.

The peculiar conversation between Nadine Janos and the Irishman, their reference to a "spy", might conceivably explain Arthur Dugald's absence last night. The temple was close by, and Arthur had expressed an interest in it. What more natural than that he should simply wait until the chalet—and the temple—were quiet, the occupants asleep, and then sneak over there for a look around?

By the time she finished dressing, she ruled out

146

that convenient theory. If it had been true, why would Nadine and the Irishman talk about "files" and familiar dangers, as if they feared someone they knew well?

Kay went down the circle steps, conscious of the click-click of her sleek new half-boots and glancing over the wrought-iron rail to see what Caro Teague was up to by this time. The girl turned over on the couch, groaned and opened her eyes. She appeared to be in much the same dazed state as Kay had found herself an hour earlier.

"Oh—Mrs. Aronson! I'm so sorry!" Caro Teague scrambled up, clutching the bedclothes, then dropping them and pressing her palms to her head. "What a headache! I know I didn't drink anything after we got back from that cellar . . . did I?"

"No. Nothing like that." Kay came down to the living room, wondering briefly if Caro was putting on some kind of act, but it seemed, upon closer observation, that the girl had been given the same drug that had given Kay the nasty headache and the thirst. "Caro, are you thirsty?"

The girl stared in the direction of the kitchen in a puzzled way. "Yes, Ma'am. I am. What could it be? We only had tea; didn't we?"

"Apparently." As Kay walked across the room to the couch, she was aware of the change in the girl's stare. Caro's hazel eyes dilated oddly as they tried to focus upon the tall, trim figure of her employer. No doubt about it, Kay thought. Caro Teague had been drugged as well. And who else but Arthur Dugald was likely to drug them? Why?

She sat on the edge of the couch, wondering at

147

the girl's almost cringing attitude at her presence. "Tell me, Caro, what happened early this morning, after we finished our tea?"

"I don't understand. Didn't we all quit at the same time? You went upstairs. To bed, we—I thought. So, when I asked to trade beds with Mr. Dugald, he agreed and I curled up here."

"And Mr. Dugald?"

Caro looked at her in limpid innocence. "But I thought he slept in the back bedroom upstairs."

"Do you recall drinking anything after you lay down here?"

"I was asleep."

"Then you don't recall anyone giving you a drink?"

This persistence set off a sudden explosion that made Kay flinch at the girl's unexpected ferocity.

"I was asleep, I tell you. Asleep! What are you trying to do to me? Get me in trouble? I swear I went to sleep! Anything else was only dreams. Nightmares."

A bit shaken by this reaction on top of her suspicions that they both had been drugged, Kay recovered her poise with an effort. "Forgive me, Caro. I'm sure your head must ache. Mine does, too. But you spoke of nightmares. Can you remember any of the details?"

The girl pressed the heels of her palms hard against her temples again. "I don't know any. Just vague things. Tunnels and caves. And faces." She looked around nervously. "Nobody I recognized. Absolutely nobody!"

Kay gave up, got to her feet and was ready to leave when Caro murmured vaguely, "Nothing

148

but the usual nightmares. Strange faces. A white shirt . . ."

"A white shirt? Or a surgeon's smock?"

Caro looked up. "I don't remember. I'm sorry, Mrs. Aronson. I'll try and help. I can do those kitchen dishes, and make the beds. Do anything else that needs doing."

Kay thanked her, advised her to take it easy, not to rush around too much, and went and got her a glass of cold water from the kitchen faucet. When she returned with the glass and one of Edna Schallert's embroidered napkins, she was just in time to see Caro pushing something under the couch with her bare feet.

"I ran the water a little while. It should be cold," Kay said, as she offered the glass to Caro. The girl took the glass and was reaching for the napkin when it fell between their fingers. As Kay stopped to pick it up, she glanced quickly at the object under the couch. It was a simple water glass, a copy of the one in Caro's trembling hands. Caro thanked her and drank thirstily while Kay tried to make something out of this latest discovery.

. . . Now, just why did that girl lie about receiving the drink in the night? If she thought the visitor in white was part of her nightmares, she would hardly have found it necessary to hide the glass. Its presence here alone proves the reality of her "nightmare" . . .

She said casually, "I suppose Mr. Dugald left early. He's a great one for those dawn walks."

Caro shrugged. "I must have been dead to the world. I never heard a thing."

Kay looked around the shadowed room. "Well,

I think I'll go down to the village and try out the sauna and some of those intriguing health tricks at the Hot Springs." Her gaze lingered briefly on the big television console at the far side of the room. "While I'm down there, I may put in a complaint about the TV."

Caro's tousled pink head went up abruptly.

"You . . . you have some complaint about it?"

Kay laughed. "Only that it doesn't work. What else could be wrong with it?"

When she left a few minutes later, stepping out into the warm, hazy morning, she was beginning to wonder if the young woman named Carolyn Teague was quite sane. Remembering some of her own half-confidences with Dugald, she amended that suspicion to add: Was anyone at Lucifer Cove entirely sane?

And she was no nearer to finding out what had happened to Leo than she had been when she left their home in Virginia.

"There has got to be someone in all this valley that I can trust. I simply haven't met the right people here."

She started out eastward, toward the temple and the main trail down into the village. There were several distant figures along the trail, most of them climbing above the cutoff path to the temple and the chalet. Probably hiking up to the little landing field on top of the mountain, she decided. Most interesting, however, was her sight of a pair, male and female, cutting into the main trail. They were obviously the big Irishman and the devil's priestess.

Kay slowed her steps, wondering if they had any servants or any acolytes at work in the little

150

Greek Temple while they were gone. The place looked deserted. She spent a few minutes making a casual study of the wild flowers bordering the steep mountainside, but when Nadine and her boyfriend had disappeared down the first sharp turn in the trail, she went up the wide steps and crossed the portico between the slender, graceful pillars. Her luck had been unexpectedly good, but at the double doors it failed her. The doors were locked.

She considered making a respectable retreat, but no one seemed to have noticed her so far. She looked behind her and found nothing except the empty path, the steep mountainside below and the village wreathed in sulphur trails from the distant Hot Springs. There was no harm in admiring the exterior of the pretty little Greek building. If she was caught she would fall back on the excuse of its architectural delights.

She walked around the building, curious about the possibility of seeing the interior without the shadow of Nadine Janos with her clever little tricks that drove people like Edna's friend Hemplemeier—and maybe Leo—to suicide. Kay had a general idea that the interior of the temple would be full of eccentricities, tricks, trapdoors, weird lighting, all the necessities for scaring her devotees into large contributions. There were no doors on the west side of the temple, and the windows appeared to be barricaded from the inside. The walls were suddenly forbidding, an ancient tomb, a grey, austere stone hint of what she would find within.

The rear of the little temple was quite another matter, tucked against the steep, rising mountain slope, and presenting a delightful haphazard look, illustrated by a kind of lean-to made of wood. She could see when she looked in the dirty window that it was filled to its tin roof with boxes, materials and other unused junk from Nadine Janos' stage effects. She walked around the lean-to with some difficulty, squeezing into the narrow aisle of earth and shale between the lean-to and the mountainside. Pebbles and burrs and dried branches from the thickets on the mountainside above kept rolling down across her feet.

Just as she crossed to the east wall of the temple, she found the rear door. It had apparently been closed in a hurry, the door still on the latch and not completely locked. She was not used to housebreaking, and hesitated briefly after she had opened the door, closed it quietly behind her and found herself in some kind of murky passage, with the lean-to's doorway at her back and several closed doors ahead of her on the east side of the passage. The entire temple was small enough so that there couldn't be more than three or four small rooms, hardly more than cubicles, behind the auditorium of the temple at the front of the building.

There was still no noise. The silence was eerie and unsettling to her. The stonework of the facade made the closed temple almost soundproof. The priestess could pull any of her little tricks in here and be unsuspected and unheard outside. Kay wondered where the illumination came from and then saw a faint blue glow at the far end of the passage where a door opened up onto what seemed to be a stage. Probably the altar, she thought wryly, and started through the passage.

The side doors opened into dressing rooms, smelling of costumes and dust, perfumes and sweat. She couldn't make out the other objects, though there seemed to be a couch in one, with flowered white sheets partially visible, the vermillion flowers gleaming in the semi-darkness like gouts of fresh blood.

Kay shuddered at the picture in her mind and closing the door, moved on quickly. She left the other doors closed and avoided them, but the queer little sick-sweet odor of that first room followed her. She had appeared in amateur plays in college, and was familiar with the odor of used and long-sealed costumes, but the suggestiveness of the costumes here seemed especially chilling. Devil worship might be absurd, even harmless to most people, but there must be some, on the edge of being unbalanced, who would find in all this mumbo-jumbo a ghostly and blasphemous reality. And the scent of those costumes pursuing her in the grey dark was strong enough, she thought, to turn even a level-headed, modern agnostic into a believer.

A believer of what? Of witches and devils? Of one all-consuming, monstrous power that toyed with lives before it destroyed souls?

She was so angry at her own deliberate inciting of horror that she laughed at her own idiotic—and fleeting—thought. But the notes of that laugh returned to her in blistering little echoes from the high roof of the temple. She had nearly reached the edge of the passage by this time, so it was too late to retrace her steps and sneak back out the rear door in a cowardly way that would delight the soul of the devil's priestess.

Having already betrayed her presence by her laugh, she studied the temple's long, narrow auditorium from behind the partially opened door. The place looked like the nave of a small country church and she was surprised to find out how very innocent the place looked, upon first glance. There seemed to be nothing dangerous hidden in that dark, empty room. But how could one be sure? There were so many corners where the light did not reach. So much darkness.

"Here goes," she told herself and stepped up onto the dais facing the auditorium. The blue glow which had led her here turned out to be a night light dangling from the rafters to a point about three yards above a lectern to the right of the dais door. On closer inspection she decided the lectern was a pulpit of sorts, used by the preacher for the various tricks of her trade, including pounding the pulpit to shake up her congregation.

Prominent in catching the light overhead was an onyx object that looked like an oversized "X". It cast weird blue shadows over her and she went across the dais to examine it. She was shocked, though hardly surprised to discover that it was actually a crucifix set upside down on the pulpit. The petty blasphemy of the coven.

Having reached for the crucifix, Kay pulled her hand back as if it had been burned, yet there was nothing to the crucifix except the chill, smooth, onyx. She must be more superstitious, or more religious, than she had thought!

A number of dangling black objects near the east wall frightened her momentarily, but the air stirred, probably as a result of her opening and closing of doors, and when she heard their metallic little rustle, she realized they must be a part of Nadine Janos' sound effects to frighten the natives.

She had looked out upon the empty auditorium—not even any pews!—and examined the dais and the lectern used by the priestess as a pulpit. During these minutes she became gradually more sensitive to a curious manifestation behind her. There was a faint chill upon her neck. The same stirring of air, no doubt, that caused the microphones and other equipment to tinkle now, as if under a giant's breath. She found herself stiffening, reluctant to turn around. When she did so, the blue overhead light swayed and one of its flareups caught and illuminated the wall behind the dais.

The wall was black. She saw nothing. If this was the altar, it must depend upon the overwrought imagination of the coven for its effects. She closed her eyes, opened them and was curious with herself for having done so. An extraordinary thing had happened. The black velvet wall hanging remained as before, or seemed to, but in the center, its darkness faintly yielded to lights, a somber glow, the color of rubies.

She stared, seeing in those somber eyes watching her with the pitiless indifference of an element, a fire, or a storm. She took a quick, backward step, crashed into the corner of the lectern-pulpit. She closed her eyes, gasping at the sudden sharp pain over her ribs, and held onto the lectern while she recovered her breath from the shock.

She leaned against the lectern, with the pressure upon her elbows, aware of a nausea and weakness that infused her body like tainted blood coursing through her veins. Strange thoughts came to her, negative and terrible in their depressing effect upon her.

. . . Leo had been going insane. He had nightmares because of that fear. He came here to be cured because there is a Spa, a clinic. The works . . . He got scared when they couldn't help him; so he left here too quickly. Maybe the plane took off without sufficient checking and preparation. My trip here was all for nothing. I've gotten like Leo. I'm beginning to imagine things. Am I going mad as he did? . . .

She had never known such depression. Life ahead, beyond this point in time, seemed futile. Pointless.

She found herself staring up at the blue light swinging overhead. She hadn't noticed before the heavy chain from which the light was suspended. The end of the chain hung below the light. Almost within reach of a tall woman. A looped chain, large as a noose.

Absurd thought . . . a noose.

. . . I believe I can reach it. I can! Simple, really, when you put your mind to it. I had no idea I was so athletic. How do people do these things? They stand on something. And then kick it out from under their feet . . .

There was a black stool over near the steps leading down off the dais to the floor of the auditorium. She took it and set it under the looped chain. Every movement seemed simple and in proper order. She stepped up on the stool, raised her arms and drew down the chain, looping it around her neck.

ELEVEN

The blue obscurity of the long room was suddenly shattered by a scream so shrill, so hideous, the macabre scene dissolved for Kay into a ghastly joke. She swayed on the narrow stool, looked around vaguely, wondered if she was still walking in some nightmare.

"Stop! Please—stop!" a woman's voice cried to her down the length of the auditorium, and as Kay let go of the chain, her arms shaking, she muttered hoarsely,

"Who are you? I can't see you."

The intruder had been running. She stopped abruptly in the pool of blue light below the dais, an astonishingly beautiful woman with a halo of deep gold hair and a sad, strange expression that shadowed her fine eyes. She was very likely in her mid-thirties, but there was an ageless quality about her that made her as terrifying to Kay as everything else about this temple of demons.

Kay looked down at her, bewildered. "Am I dreaming? What is wrong? Why was I? . . ."

"I think you must have been hypnotized," the

157

woman said gently. "It's the combination of lights and other atmospheric tricks here. I am Christine Deeth. I . . . live at the Spa. Let me help you."

Something in Kay revolted at the offer of help from one of *them*. For all she knew, this pale beauty standing in that weird blue pool of light was just another member of a group that seemed determined to drive her out of the Cove, or into madness. They had made a very good beginning. She glanced up at the chain and shuddered.

"I may owe you something more than thanks," she admitted, stepping off the dais with the help of the woman's outstretched hand.

Christine Deeth's flesh was not cold or clammy as Kay half expected, in view of the way she suddenly materialized out of that sinister dark, but the woman was actually as shaken and nervous as Kay. That did surprise her.

"Do you mean to tell me I was hypnotized into trying to—to do that incredible thing?" Kay asked as they hurried through the auditorium, away from that altar and its horrible memories. "Who hypnotized me? I was alone in there. I'm sure I was alone. Who would do such a thing?" She steeled herself to look back, knowing if she didn't, she would be forever afraid of creeping things behind her.

The black altar cloth was perfectly blank as before. The blue light swung listlessly above the lectern. Its chain glimmered in that depressing blue glow.

"Ghastly! I can't believe it happened. Mrs. Deeth, who hypnotized me?" Kay took a deep, full breath of daylight as the woman turned the thumb bolt on the doors and opened the right door quietly, with enormous care not to make any sound. Mrs. Deeth did not reply to Kay's question, perhaps because she did not know the answer. Or maybe because she didn't want to.

"Mrs. Deeth?"

"Please call me Christine. Everyone does. I suppose you will be wanting to rest now. And no one will blame you if you take the first plane out of here."

Kay looked sharply at her. "Does everyone leave here on the first plane?"

Christine Deeth seemed surprised that her simple expression had been questioned. "No. Many people come by bus. Or drive in. Some even walk in."

"And how do they leave?"

The woman's lips moved as if she had started to speak and lost her voice. She looked up at the hazy sky, and then walked over to the edge of the path and stared down over the valley shrouded in acrid yellow fumes of sulphur.

"You must understand, Mrs. Aronson, people make their own choice in coming here. Because of that, many prefer to remain at the Cove . . . for various inducements."

"If they can afford it," Kay remarked skeptically, remembering Caro Teague's desperate anxiety to keep her job. "But that doesn't explain the extraordinary thing that happened to me. I am not a depressive. Nor am I suicidal. I don't believe my own suicide ever crossed my mind."

Mrs. Deeth murmured in a nervous, hesitant voice, "Perhaps . . . subconsciously?"

"Not subconsciously, or unconsciously. And it

has always seemed to me the height of cruelty to others, to hang oneself. Heaven knows there are pills. Drugs. All sorts of ways for these things to be handled. But hanging! Ugh! Who did that to me?"

When, once again, Mrs. Deeth evaded the answer, Kay saw that there was no point in pursuing the matter. She did not trust Mrs. Deeth either. It seemed obvious to Kay now that some kind of hypnotism explained other horrors here, the suicides, possibly even Leo's behavior. But what intelligence was behind it? Could a woman like Nadine Janos mastermind such powerful hypnoses?

Kay was starting down the trail to the valley and Mrs. Deeth had no choice but to go with her. The woman's thin fingers worked nervously as Kay watched them out of the corner of her eyes. Mrs. Deeth was divorced, Caro said, and she wore no wedding ring, but on her ring finger she did wear an extraordinary band of white, either platinum or gold. The important thing was the tiny platinum and onyx setting with twin amber stones.

Amber stones like eyes, Kay thought. And onyx striped the platinum background. A cat. A cat that could almost be an animal she had seen. Kinkajou. . . .

Kay took a deep breath and became all friendliness, all naivete and trust.

"My husband used to adore cats. I can see you do, too."

"Well, I like them, but . . ." Christine Deeth followed her gaze, glanced at her own hands and belatedly understood. "This is different. It is from a close friend. A kind of . . ."

"Engagement ring?"

To Kay's surprise Christine said softly, "A wedding ring." She raised the ring finger and touched her cheek with the exquisite, if slightly sinister cat-wedding ring. The caress of the ring against her cheek indicated a depth of feeling over which Kay was exceedingly curious. "I saw the Cove's pet cat yesterday when it was almost killed by a dog, up here on the mountain." She watched the woman's reaction, but it was clear that the fight was no news to Christie Deeth.

"Yes," she said. "He came to me—the cat, Kinkajou—for help and the doctor and I put on salves, did our best."

"The extraordinary thing is that he seems so well today."

Mrs. Deeth smiled faintly. "He has excellent recuperative powers. And then, to cover the scars, he always wears a—"

Incredulous, Kay repeated, "He *wears?*"

"A . . . a collar. Yes. A collar."

"But a collar couldn't possibly conceal those scars. They cover his entire throat." Seeing that the woman had become agitated, Kay changed the subject, but reserved in a corner of her brain these added notes of suspicion. Aloud, she said with a pleasant gesture at the mountains, "This is such a lovely place. I wish Leo had been able to enjoy it before he left so suddenly."

"Oh, no! Mr. Aronson hated . . ." Mrs. Deeth bit her lip. "He liked the cool days better. You see, he'd been here years ago, when he first came to America. I'm told he couldn't even speak English when he arrived. He learned so much here. He owed to—to the Cove a great deal of his later success in life."

Kay remembered suddenly the discussions she had with Arthur Dugald. He had come close to guessing much the same thing. Or, at least, he indicated it was a guess. "When Leo came to America and to this place, who taught him, prepared him for that jungle world outside? He was a good pupil, but who could have been so incredibly brilliant that he could teach a man like Leo?"

"But, of course, it was . . ." This time Kay had absolutely no doubt of it, Mrs. Deeth had been about to mention a name and had cut it off at the last second. "It must have been some bright financier who specialized in the field and saw in Mr. Aronson an apt pupil."

"And forced my husband to return thirty years later to a place he loathed."

Mrs. Deeth looked at her, greatly troubled. "Please don't talk like this in the village. It might reach the wrong ears. You saw today what the power of suggestion can do, even to a woman of strong mind like yourself."

They were crossing the plank bridge over the dry creek bed and several youthful hikers passed them, going up the trail with loaded canvas bags on their backs, the bags adorned by tin plates and cups. Kay lowered her voice, quite ready to believe Christine Deeth was right about the danger, but also aware that she was getting closer to the truth she had come here to discover. The trouble was, in spite of its obvious danger, she had to pursue the matter to its conclusion. Otherwise, Leo might have died for nothing and others would go his way.

"Did they find out how Edna Schallert died?" she asked suddenly.

"A heart attack, I believe. She—poor Edna— was exploring that tunnel through the mountain. It is rather like a chain of caves and occasionally parts of it are used for storing things, liquors and things of that sort. Also, it is possible Edna was making her way to the village, and felt that the tunnels might be a short-cut. The trail is rather steep for a woman of Edna's age."

"Where does the tunnel come out?"

Christine looked at her frankly. "I've never been in it. I get claustrophobia at the whole idea of caves. But Marc—Mr. Meridon tells me it has several exits. One of them near the parking lot in back of the Spa. Probably several on the east side of the valley, near the Hot Springs. It is not precisely a tunnel, as I understand it, but a series of caves, like those they call the Pinnacles, over the mountain near Hollister." She sighed. "It was a great blow about Edna. She was responsible for my coming to Lucifer Cove in the first place. I'd had a traumatic divorce—entirely my fault—and Edna talked me into coming here to recuperate. Now, of course, I can hardly remember any other life before I came here."

"It is rather like being a prisoner, I should imagine. And you must hate the forces that keep you here."

"Oh, no! Quite the contrary! It isn't hate. It is love that keeps me here."

. . . She is certainly brainwashed, Kay thought grimly, and resolved not to trust her, no matter

163

what the woman had done to save her. "It certainly wasn't love that brought Leo back. He hated the very thought of it. Arthur believes it was Leo's dread of being summoned here that caused his terrible nightmares."

"Who is Arthur?" Mrs. Deeth asked with a certain sharpness that puzzled Kay.

"Leo's secretary. Arthur Dugald. The only man close to him. Arthur accompanied Leo everywhere. But on this last trip Leo refused to let either of us come until he had arranged things. I wonder what that arrangement entailed."

"A new deal, I expect. He hoped to renew his contract."

"With whom?" Acknowledging to herself a quickened heartbeat, Kay wondered if they were getting closer to the pinpointed truth, but once more, Christie Deeth became evasive.

"The—the management."

"And he was hypnotized into ordering up his plane too soon, and killing himself and his pilot as a result." She waited for Mrs. Deeth to deny this passionately, but to her astonishment and discomfort, the woman said nothing, thus lending tacit agreement to the idea.

"But why? Why? Just because he broke some contract or other. Did he refuse to pay some debt? Was that it?"

"I believe so," Mrs. Deeth agreed vaguely.

"But Leo could pay any debt. And if he had trouble meeting the deadline, he might have asked me to help. It couldn't have been a question of money."

"Principles. As I understand it, the matter came to a question of principles. But no one literally murdered him, Mrs. Aronson. I must make that plain to you. It was more a case of your husband's bad conscience. He denied the debt, and became nervous, perhaps slipshod in his nervousness. And insisted on flying out before the plane was ready. There was no last check. And so they died, your husband and his pilot. Here we are. The Spa. Were you coming to breakfast here? Or lunch, as it seems to be past noon."

"No. I think not. I have a little score to settle with the doctor who runs the Hot Springs."

Christie protested worriedly, "I wouldn't wander around the Hot Springs if I were you. It's a labyrinth if you don't know the way to the proper offices."

"Thank you. I'll be careful." Kay watched the woman with her lovely lost look, go into the mirrored and paneled entrance hall of the Spa, and gradually seem to dissolve in that darkness.

"Curious that she arrived just in time at that Devil's Temple to stop me," Kay thought. "Not that I would have gone through with it, of course. I was only examining the possibilities of inducing people to commit suicide. I would never have done such a ghastly thing ... would I?"

How had Christine Deeth happened to be there? It was almost as if she had come seeking someone, and not finding him or her, had done the next best thing, saved a stranger from a most involuntary suicide.

"Lucky for me," Kay admitted with a shudder. "And with all this chit-chat I've forgotten to ask about Edna Schallert's funeral. They must know something in there."

She went into the hall and heard voices in the

165

reception office almost immediately. First, there was the giggling, high-pitched voice of the curvacious young blonde, Bonnie Lou Bryer. But it was the voice of the male with whom she was flirting that jarred Kay. Arthur Dugald seemed to be jollier, lighter than he had been in Leo's service. He was teasing the girl about being beautiful but dumb and she was denying, prettily.

" 'Course I know. I work there; don't I? Call me dumb and the rest of it just because parts of the damn springs are out of bounds to employees. And believe you me, sweetie, I don't go sneaking around those areas to make out with something male."

And then Arthur's voice, surprisingly warm. Almost, Kay thought, almost too warm to be real. "But I'm sure anyone as pretty as you, Bonnie Lou, is going to be pursued through the sacred white halls of Lucifer Cove Hot Springs."

"That's silly, Hon. When I want to—that is, if I wanted to take a roll in the hay, I'd go into one of the rooms in the pink sector. Or the lilac one. I'd never go rushing down into the—" She giggled. "—the bowels of the Hot Springs. Not for any guy."

What was Arthur Dugald getting at? It seemed an extraordinary conversation for Arthur, though, in all likelihood, he was fishing for information. She found herself passionately anxious that he should be gathering facts on Leo's side, not against his side, and hers.

"Were you waiting to speak with the receptionist?" asked a quiet voice behind Kay. "Perhaps I can help you, Mrs. Aronson."

Kay was embarrassed enough about all her

166

eavesdropping since her arrival in the Cove, without being caught at it by Marc Meridon, whose good opinion she desired. She swung around, managed to recover face enough to say quickly, "Yes, I think you may. I came to find out when Edna Schallert's funeral will be held. And where?"

The two in the reception room stopped talking. Marc, who looked tired and rather pale, but no less attractive, regarded Kay with the first real sympathy she had encountered in Lucifer Cove. "I'm afraid Miss Schallert's will required that she be buried with the rest of her family, in a cemetery in San Mateo County. Her body was removed from the valley early this morning. The funeral is probably taking place at this very moment."

Someone must be a very rapid embalmer! Kay found herself believing him, in spite of her common sense. "Then I think I will walk up to the Hot Springs. I want to find out what drug Dr. Rossiter gave me in the night."

Marc's eyes flashed. He suddenly looked dangerous and Kay flinched in surprise. But the instant he saw her reaction, he apologized and she was swayed by the unexpected warmth of his smile.

"Please, forgive me. But we've tried to make things as pleasant as possible for you, partly because I—because we like you and partly too, because we owe it to you. Somehow, without intending to, we are involved in your mind with Mr. Aronson's death. And we can never repay you or the world for that loss."

"Thank you." Whatever the guilt of someone at

167

Lucifer Cove, Marc, at least, was willing to acknowledge the connection. He offered his hand along with that special smile and she put her own fingers in his. "I believe you. But I don't need people feeding me drugs. I really can do some things for myself."

"I agree. You say Dr. Rossiter administered you a drug. You didn't ask for one? It does seem excessive to give you a drug when every client who arrives at the Cove is given his own, or her own silver pill box, with every capsule, every pill, you could possibly have occasion for."

Arthur Dugald had come to the doorway and was looking at Kay in an odd way. She didn't know what he was trying to tell her, but she was very much aware that he had access both to the drugs in her own silver pill box, and to her water glass and that of Caro Teague. Her own personal feeling for him did not detract from the circumstantial evidence.

"I'm sure you're right about the doctor," she told Marc, "but I'd like to go up and talk to him, all the same."

"Happy to escort you, Mrs. Aronson," Arthur Dugald spoke up suddenly. "I like to earn my pay." Knowing him so well, she thought he sounded worried. Probably she was getting too close to pinning him down.

Fortunately, Marc cut in to assure one and all, "There is no reason to put anyone out. I have to go up to the Hot Springs on business. I may save you considerable wandering around. Since the fire last summer we have had people getting lost now and then. Shall we go, Mrs. Aronson?"

When they were leaving together, Kay looked

back and saw that Arthur Dugald had returned to his teasing flirtation with Bonnie Lou Bryer, but she could not be wrong about one thing. Over Bonnie Lou's bright head he was watching Kay and Marc with great concentration.

"What am I going to do?" she thought desperately. "I've got to trust someone."

TWELVE

When they passed a Regency front white shop with what appeared to be a hairy gargoyle peering out at them through the small-paned windows, Marc mentioned that it was Mrs. Peasecod's shop, and Kay finally placed the gargoyle. It must be the old witch-like character she had met the day before at the Sea-Green Pool. The woman who had been responsible for her new wardrobe. The woman seemed inordinately proud of her acquaintance with Marc Meridon.

Kay thought ruefully, "And she's not the only one." She was deeply conscious of the man beside her. Though the flesh of his thin hand had been cool when he touched her fingers, she found herself speculating now upon the probable warmth of his lips. In her own circumstances, only a matter of weeks after Leo's death, she despised this purely physical weakness she had apparently developed for a man who was virtually a stranger. Besides, unless he was the male who had made the compact with her husband thirty years ago and taught Leo everything Leo came to know—

incredible for a man who looked scarcely thirty now—Marc was about five years too young for her.

"What did you and my husband talk about that hour or two you were together? The day before he died."

He glanced at her. She did not look; so she didn't know or guess what he was thinking about her.

"We talked about your husband's distinguished career."

She had it on the tip of her tongue to ask him if he had known her husband at the beginning of Leo's fabulous career. But she found it impossible. It would make Marc Meridon sixty at the very least. Absolutely impossible. He hadn't even any wrinkles, except shadows beneath those remarkable eyes and perhaps . . . it seemed to her that she remembered a scar beneath his chin, or just below it. She wanted to look but didn't dare. Besides, he was wearing another of those especially flattering scarves today.

"Here we are."

She looked up. They were at the big gates which had opened like faithful magic eyes as Marc and Kay entered. The grounds had a little too much sulphur trailing in long strings across the air but this didn't keep the outdoor pool, naturally heated, from being crowded with young people and several not so young women.

"I had no idea there were so many people in this valley," she remarked, looking around to see if she recognized anyone.

"It seems to be the popularity center. Dulane

used to say we asphyxiated our most loyal clientele."

"Who?"

"Our most loyal clientele."

"No! I mean—what name did you mention just now?"

She was sure he hesitated deliberately, but he had begun to point out the path to the reception center, in the middle of the two-story sprawling series of buildings, which all joined each other in haphazard fashion.

"You can't lose your way if you concentrate on the secret. The marigolds lead to the gold sector. Simply follow the line of color and the arrows low on the wall, near the floor. This simplifies it for all nationalities, all people of different tongues. They can understand the directions by following the color to their destination."

Impressed, she said, "I noticed in the parking lot that there were licenses from all over the world. It is astonishing, the business you do."

"Not really. We offer very tempting inducements."

She persisted, "What was the name of the man who joked about you asphyxiating the people with sulphur?"

"Dulane," he said casually. "A client some years ago."

He was protecting Arthur. No question about it. Would he protect Arthur against her suspicion that he might have drugged her and Caro? How could he defend both Arthur and Dr. Rossiter at the same time? Fascinating as he might be, she wished she could be alone to make a phone call to Detroit and check on Arthur, once and for all.

People stopped whatever they were doing and looked at them as Marc and Kay passed. She was keenly aware of the interest they took in Marc Meridon. It was surprising that a young man his age could arouse such respect.

Then he ushered her into the gold passage, the direct way to the central reception desk, explaining that they must then go to the second floor receiving area in a large hall.

"Remember, you mustn't wander around here alone. The clinic was burned in the fire last summer, and some rebuilding has taken place in the lower areas; disposal areas, et cetera. The beauty regions, the facial and body chemistry areas are on the pink corridor. But you hardly need that help, Mrs. Aronson."

She smiled but was too busy studying the building's curious interior to pay much attention to his small talk.

The ceilings were high and neon-lighted. The walls of white with only those faint identifying arrows near the floor made her think of hospitals and then of morgues. At the center desk where several passages veered off to cardinal points on the compass a woman was seated, with a complexion so flawless and eyes so expressionless she might have been a carefully uniformed department store mannequin. Her eyelids flickered at the sight of Marc and Kay, but even to him she did not venture a smile. It might crack what was probably her new face.

If this was the rejuvenation work Dr. Rossiter had come down to after his great experiments in transplants, it was no wonder he was embittered.

"Miss Idwel, we are here to see Dr. Rossiter,"

said Marc in his pleasant way, with only the faintest suggestion of authority. "Mrs. Aronson is a new client."

"Briefly," said Kay with a look just as haughty as the up-and-down superior glance of Miss Idwel.

"Of course," Miss Idwel agreed, and then when she had motioned them on, Kay was sure she heard the woman mutter, "Aren't they all?"

It put Kay on guard again with the knowledge that people had one intention when they entered Lucifer Cove and apparently were persuaded to change that intention.

She and Marc stepped into a tiny elevator with glamorous pink satin padded walls that defeated their reassuring purpose by giving her a sound case of claustrophobia. They were the sort of thing she would expect of a very posh padded cell in a lunatic ward.

They made so brief a trip on the miniature elevator that Kay was unprepared for the second floor arrival when they stepped out. The reception area here included a desk chair on a small platform, surrounded on three sides by desks and files. Of all people, Thalia Cates was the receptionist, her harsh features clashing noticeably with the pink satin surroundings. She seemed a little upset at Kay's arrival, either because of her crush on Marc Meridon, or even, absurdly enough, because the newspaperwoman was embarrassed to be caught working as a receptionist rather than as a writer.

Kay tried to be friendly enough to gloss over the difficulty. "Good morning, Mrs. Cates. Or is it good afternoon by now? It's good to see a friend, after so many unfamiliar faces."

Mrs. Cates perked up at that and grinned, showing almost an excessive amount of teeth, like a huge dog with a terrifying grin.

"How've you been, Luv? Find the right connections here, and all?"

Marc excused himself and disappeared down one of the corridors to find out if Dr. Rossiter was in his office or in the midst of work that would not allow him to be disturbed.

"Like making a new face for some old bat," Thalia explained knowingly to Kay. She looked over her shoulder, saw that Marc was out of sight. "How d'you like this place? Kooky, isn't it?"

"All of that," Kay agreed. "I suppose you know we found Edna Schallert last night."

"Rotten thing. Yes. Through the grapevine. It always gives the rest of us a case of the shakes. You should have seen the drug take go up this morning. Barbiturates, bennies, dexies, hard stuff. Everybody's loaded."

Startled, Kay asked why. "The woman had a bad heart. It wasn't unexpected."

"*Comme ci comme ca.*" Thalia Cates shrugged, the gesture calling attention to the huge red freckles on her shoulders that could be seen beneath the silky dacron of her uniform. "Here at the Cove it's 'the bell tolls for thee.' 'Each man's death diminishes me.' You know the bit."

"Good heavens! I'd leave if I felt that way."

Thalia looked dubious at this perfectly natural advice.

"Easier said than done. We're all in hock up to

175

our fritters. Not—" She added hastily, "—that I've got any money problems, thank—thanks be! I'm only taking over this desk temporarily. For atmosphere, you know. To write a series on the people who pass through these files. In one file, out the other, you might say." She gazed at Kay curiously. "What you doing here? Change of hair? Makeup? Not a face life! You need a face lift like I need another chin. But those laugh lines could use a teeny smidgen of silicone, maybe."

Kay smiled with a conscious effort. "I'm just here to discuss something with Dr. Rossiter. About—about Miss Schallert's death."

"Uh-uh. Don't get too curious, Hon. Remember what happened to Alice when she fell down the rabbit hole. Too many questions." She grinned uneasily. "Don't say I didn't warn you."

Marc's voice said cheerfully, "Warn her of what, Mrs. Cates? Well, the doctor will be returning any minute. Are you ready, Mrs. Aronson?"

To Kay's surprise, Thalia Cates held out a wrinkled, mottled hand. "Take care."

"Thank you." Kay returned the friendly handshake, puzzled by the woman's warning. They had only met once before and Kay couldn't recall that she had been nice enough to the columnist to warrant this consideration. It was especially odd when, in spite of that warning, Thalia Cates turned around and fluttered over Marc Meridon with every youthful feminine wile she could think of. Probably her warning had been an attempt to keep Kay away from Meridon.

Marc suggested, "You might wait in Rossiter's office. You will find it more comfortable."

At the moment Kay did not understand why

Thalia Cates flashed such an astonished look, until she found herself inside the office itself. There was little comfort and a great deal of austere efficiency about the room. There were a number of little Egyptian tabarets with bronze tray tops around the room. Under the north window whose drapes were closed, there was a display table. Under the glass were numerous coins, some doubtless exhibited for their rarity and worth, others for their beauty. But all must be worth many fortunes. On the bronze trays were other tempting tidbits. On one was the huge parchment menu of the Cove's dining salon. On another was a ticker-tape and beneath it magazines turned to stock market pages which had a peculiar habit of showing a rising market.

There were other tempting areas, like a catalogue of women's clothing which could be obtained at Mrs. Peasecod's remarkable shop. Temptations for everyone. No matter what the desire or mood. Kay passed them all and sat down in a stiff chair facing the doctor's desk. Marc had gone out into the hall and suddenly Kay heard Dr. Rossiter's voice, irritated, impatient.

"I was in the middle of my work. I can't afford to be interrupted. You know that. What damnable thing is this?"

Kay sat up self-consciously. This was going to be an unpleasant session. Dr. Rossiter came into the room, still in his white smock which had a bloodstain no wider than a hair running across the breast of the smock. His dark hair was unruly, his deep-set eyes looking tired but zealous for whatever work so enthralled him. Marc, behind him, shrugged and grimaced at Kay. The doctor made an obvious effort to be civil.

"Good afternoon, Mrs. Aronson. I hope there were no after effects from your discovery last night."

"There was one rather bad after effect, Doctor."

He had gone over to his desk but raised his head and stared at her now. She could have sworn he was startled.

"How do you mean? Was someone else made ill?"

"Both Miss Teague and I were drugged."

Instead of looking guilty or surprised, he glanced at Marc with disgust. "I told you before that it is a mistake to allow free access to barbiturates and the rest. It is not the way to break up the temptation to drugs."

Marc tried to be reasonable. "The theory is that prohibition makes the object more desirable."

"Absurd theory! So you and Miss Teague took too large a dose of some drug. Is that it?"

Kay said icily, "No, Doctor. It is not. Mr. Meridon, may I speak to the doctor in private about the symptoms and about Miss Teague's condition?"

"Of course. Forgive me. I'll be along presently, Mrs. Aronson. Doctor, you will show Mrs. Aronson every courtesy?"

"Certainly. Certainly." There was so much impatience in the doctor's tone and manner that Kay found it extremely difficult to believe he had actually drugged her and Caro Teague. He would be much too busy over his own affairs.

When Marc left the room he carefully closed the door. Kay said nothing until his footsteps receded along the hall. Doctor Rossiter, meanwhile, leaned over his desk, making notes on a squared pad in a quick, black scrawl. Kay moved closer to the desk.

"Doctor, would you tell me something, quite honestly?"

He frowned but as he threw down his pen and faced her, she sensed once more that whatever his concerns were at Lucifer Cove, he was not going around drugging strange women, unless it would aid his experiments in some way.

"I will tell you whatever I can. Do you by any chance imagine I drugged you last night?"

"Did you?"

The directness of her reply made him smile slightly. She was impressed at the almost, though not quite human aspect of his tight-skinned face.

"No."

"Then who did?"

"Your friend Dugald. Probably to protect you from following him into some danger. Why did you believe I was responsible?"

Why had she picked him? She thought back and remembered the flash of white both she and Caro had seen. She told him so. He nodded and gazed thoughtfully at his fingernails, repeating.

"I suggest you look closer to home."

She stood abruptly. "That's ridiculous! Why would Arthur want to drug us? And what about the white smock?"

"A white shirt, for example?"

She wished he were not so convincing.

"Did you treat my husband when he was in the valley?"

"No."

She had to laugh. "I can't pump you; can I?"

"Not today. I am more than usually busy."

"Do you know anything about hypnotism?"

He looked at her curiously. "Very little. It's effects have been vastly overrated."

"Then I won't keep you." She got up and went to the door. Marc was nowhere in sight. Thalia Cates was huddled over her desk, busily going through a series of files. Doing a little spying on her own, thought Kay with some amusement.

The hall to the left of the doctor's office was deserted but at the turn in the hall, she saw something shadowed and dark, possibly Marc Meridon's gray-striped suede jacket. She went down the hall, but found she had been mistaken. Nothing was there except a staircase and a continuance of the hall. The shadow had been cast by the staircase light. Of the two she preferred the staircase which would lead her down to the first floor and, she hoped, escape from this eerie place that seemed suspended between two worlds, the living and the dead. She did not want to be in the creepy place any longer than necessary.

She was halfway down the stairs when she heard a sound and stopped, shivering. It was the long, curving howl of a hound, announcing the presence of death to the superstitious. It hardly seemed possible but the animal must be inside the building. She panicked and began to run the rest of the way. There was a door opening off the first landing. She had almost missed it.

She tried the door latch and when it opened,

she pushed out of the staircase, finding herself in a small room hardly larger than a closet. There were no windows. One small electric light swung overhead, but Kay had very little interest in that. She was intent upon the covered object on the plinth under the light.

Her hands trembled so that she couldn't at first roll the sheet away from what she suspected was a human body. Beneath the sheet, the body was sewed into a shroud, but there was a plastic tag suspended on red plastic thread that made a ghastly necklace for the head beneath the shroud.

EDNA MYRTLE SCHALLERT
#1818-69-71
NO OUTSIDE CONNECTIONS
FOR FURNACE DISPOSAL

There would be no funeral for Edna Schallert. She would be just one more part of the daily disposal of rubbish at the Hot Springs.

Kay pressed both her hands to her mouth. She thought she would scream, but with an enormous effort, she refrained and shakily rearranged the sheet and tag.

THIRTEEN .

It was too late to interfere with the burial of Edna Schallert. She was dead and had no apparent relatives. None who would wonder because she had no funeral, possibly not even a burial plot. Kay wondered where they buried their dead at Lucifer Cove. They had lied to her, intimating that the funeral would be held elsewhere. Marc had specifically lied to her.

"What will happen to her estate? I must ask someone. Very casually." She assumed the main reason people like Edna were welcomed here was for their estates. But that suggested that Edna Schallert and others like her were murdered. Had they intended to murder Leo at the Cove, before his hurried departure?

Arthur was sure Edna had simply died of a heart attack. But Arthur was probably part of the evil doings in this place. And it could have been Arthur's white shirt, not the smock of Dr. Rossiter that she and Caro had seen in the night. The reason seemed obvious. Someone didn't want the women interfering or asking embarrassing questions when Edna Schallert's body was removed. Or, possibly, Arthur hadn't wanted the women prowling around after him early this morning when he did his own prowling.

Yes. It all went back to Arthur Dugald. She had a sinking feeling of disappointment, as if the floor had suddenly dropped out beneath her feet.

She didn't know whether to go on down the stairs into—God knew what—or retrace her steps and simply walk up to Mrs. Cates, announcing that she was lost. She went out on the landing, still undecided, but suddenly aware of noises somewhere below the landing. Footsteps, shuffling and heavy.

Kay waited no longer but hurried up the steps to the second floor. She had nearly reached Dr. Rossiter's office, breathlessly, when she came upon Thalia Cates coming out of the doctor's office. The woman brightened at sight of her.

"Here you are. Kay, my dear, Mr. Meridon has been looking for you. Where on earth did you pop off to?"

"Sorry. I'm afraid I got lost. I walked around to the end of the hall. No way out. So—here I am."

Thalia must know something, too. She looked uneasy, even anxious. "No way out? No. I guess not." She returned to her desk in the center of the wide hall. "This place is kind of tangled. Especially since the fire last summer. The clinic burned and cut off a lot of these corridors."

Kay was carefully casual. "The clinic. I imagine that would have been above the disposal units."

But Mrs. Cates had clumsily dropped a handful

183

of gold-bordered white cards all over the floor under her desk and her reply was so muffled, Kay had to ask her to repeat what she had said. Marc Meridon arrived at the same time from what apparently was the pink passage.

"So this is where you disappeared to! Has everything gone well with you, Mrs. Aronson? All the little matters arranged with Dr. Rossiter?"

"Very well indeed, thank you," she said with excruciating politeness. He might be irresistibly attractive, but even his attractions could not quite ease her memory of that strange little closet-room where the dead and desiccated body of poor Edna Schallert lay waiting to be run through the Lucifer Cove grinder, the "disposal area."

"If I live to be a hundred," Kay thought, "I can never forget that tag on Miss Schallert's body, with the casual notation that set her for the disposal unit."

Marc ushered her over to the pink satin elevator and they rode down to the first floor.

"At least I am not of this hell," she thought as she walked away from the Hot Springs, along the path rimmed with cheerful marigolds. But she was deeply depressed by the realization that she couldn't trust anyone in Lucifer Cove.

First, and most important, she had to call the people in Detroit who would know about the history of labor leader Aristede Amanos and his employee, Adam Dulane. Above all, she had to discover just what Arthur's relationship was with his Detroit employer; whether he had really been responsible in any way for attacks on Amanos, or even for the labor leader's death.

The afternoon shadows were long and deep by the time Marc and Kay left the grounds of the Hot Springs.

"You must be starved," he reminded her in his sympathetic voice. "I know you have no interest in meeting our other clients in the dining salon," he laughed. "Some of them are a bit tiresome, I expect. But there is no reason why you shouldn't have a meal served to you in one of the suites at the Spa."

"You are very considerate, but I really don't need it. Not yet, at any rate. I wonder . . . is there somewhere that I might go to make a long distance call?"

Marc looked at her. She found it hard to avoid the warm regard she always felt in his eyes.

"Nothing easier. Why don't you make your call in comfort at the Spa?"

Kay thought anxiously, "And have everyone listen in, I don't doubt."

"A great idea," she said aloud. "Thank you very much."

They walked along the main street together and Kay was very much aware of the interest in the eyes of the Cove's clients. She was not so conceited as to suppose that she herself aroused this excitement and tension in the citizens of Lucifer Cove. It was her companion. And that extraordinary interest in him puzzled her, too. He appeared to be a very ordinary young man with somber, handsome dark eyes, a nice manner, and a mysterious but pervasive charm. Hardly earth-shaking; yet they all watched him as if he were the Angel Gabriel himself.

In front of the Spa's entrance the shadows

were especially thick, stabbed here and there by bolts of red-orange sunset light. For a minute Kay thought she made out Arthur Dugald's figure in the piercing light that hit the tunnel between the parking lot and the street, and she was astonishingly disappointed when the man proved to be a stranger.

Inside the Spa Marc called to a sleek young bellman named Raoul. "Show Mrs. Aronson into the Small Salon. She wishes to make a long distance telephone call. And have a tray of sandwiches brought to her."

She was surprised at how hungry she felt at the sound of those sandwiches. It was no time to think of her stomach. Nevertheless, when she went into that elegant little salon opening off the main corridor of the Spa and was given privacy plus the magic arrival of sandwiches and a pot of coffee, it was hard for her to be suspicious of anyone at the Spa.

Once more, everything was soft and flattering pink, except the marble fireplace and mantel. Kay sat down at the tiny marble sidetable, looked over the delicious assortment of sandwiches, and chose one while she took up the pink phone.

"May I have an outside line?"

She didn't hear the reply. There was quite a bit of static and presently she had her line and a voice came on.

"Santarita Beach. Long distance."

"I want to make a credit card call to a party in Detroit. I'm afraid I haven't the number."

"Yes, Ma'am. I'll try the Detroit operator. What name are you calling, Ma'am?"

"Aristede Amanos. Or anyone of that last name."

"Your own name and number, Ma'am?"

Kay sighed, gave all numerical details and waited. After much chit-chat the Santarita operator repeated what Kay had already heard. There was no one in the Detroit telephone directory by the name Amanos.

Of course not! Arthur, alias Adam Dulane, had probably murdered him long ago!

But it was easier to convince her head than her heart. Not Arthur, the quiet, reliable man whose presence in her marriage had contributed almost as much security and permanence as Leo himself. And then, the greatest mystery, If Arthur was a betrayer, a murderer, how had Leo come to trust him so completely? She had always supposed that nobody knew and understood people as well as Leo did.

She ate several of the other slender little sandwiches, one at a time, but rapidly and almost unconsciously, while she wondered what she would do. Obviously, she could not fight this evil by herself. The smart, if cowardly thing to do was to get out of the valley, and as quickly as possible. She drank the coffee, feeling a surge of heat and nervous courage with it. She had left very little of value in the chalet. She could actually leave at once. Just walk out. Or, if that seemed a trifle desperate and melodramatic, she could rent somebody's car here in the village. It would take much longer to contact Leo's company pilot in Hollister, over the eastern mountain range, and have him get the plane up for use.

She stopped, with the coffee cup only just

touching her lips. Hadn't Leo done precisely the same thing, and died as a result? The only solution was to keep her plans an absolute secret. She finished the coffee and ate another "finger" of sandwich to give her the stamina she was going to need.

Staring at the dainty telephone, she wondered how safe it would be to make the call to the man who had piloted the plane for her and Arthur Dugald. After considerable debate with herself, she took up the telephone again. There was no familiar droning sound. She clicked a few times before becoming convinced that the line was dead.

"I suppose it would be pompous of me to think they went to all the trouble of cutting the service just on my account."

Nevertheless, the act had been completed, and she couldn't call out. She looked hard at what remained of the delicious little sandwich assortment. For all she knew, they could be poisoned. Anything was possible at Lucifer Cove. And not a single soul—if there were any *souls* here—that she could trust!

She got up and was halfway across the dainty, feminine room when the salon was besieged by an Irish hurricane. Priestess Nadine Janos had a companion very like this big, dark fellow who came roaring in complaining loudly to himself of the world's injustices, and plumped his not inconsiderable length down on the elegant, pink and gold Louis Quinze couch. It was not until he turned toward the room in the midst of stretching out and reached for what remained on the silver sandwich tray that he caught sight of Kay.

"What the hell! And me thinking I was alone!" He sat up, ruffling his tousled head and grinning in a friendly way. "I'm O'Flannery, but you may call me 'Irish.' And you'll be the great Mrs. Aronson herself?"

"Herself it is," she said, mimicking his accent. "I was about to make a phone call, but the line seems to have gone dead."

He shrugged, not finding this a particularly unusual event. "Depends who calls. And where they call to." He looked up at her, his eyes clearer than his general condition. "You wanted to call Detroit and check on your husband's man."

"What! Where did you hear that?" So this honest rogue was one of them, too!

He blinked, ruffled up his hair again and made a conscious effort to throw off the effects of whatever he had been drinking. "Never you mind. I hear things. Which is the point." He looked around. In spite of his size and obvious courage, he was obviously in awe of something. "Look here. You've a mind to leave this place haven't you?" She nodded. "And how will you be doing this simple little thing?"

"I can't call the pilot of the plane that brought me here. I thought I'd rent someone's car, and get away by the Coast Highway."

He shook his head. "No dice. You won't find anybody to do it. They've got to keep you here. You know the way of things."

She bit off the angry question and asked instead," Then how do I do it?"

He considered. "Are you a good climber?"

189

"Very good. Leo used to enjoy hiking, and I kept up quite well."

"Then that's it. Take the offshoot of the caves that pierce the east range. You'll find yourself coming out on the mountain above one of the valley hamlets. Near Hollister."

"And I can pick up my pilot there," she added thoughtfully. "It just might work. How do I reach those caves you are talking about? Do they begin under the chalet?"

Irish finished off Kay's coffee. "Not unless you have a thing for tunnels. You'll be finding the eastern caves just off the main trail up to the meadow on the mountaintop. There's a cave opening, kind of camouflaged by a lot of brush."

"How will I know where to start looking for the cave opening?"

He got up, untangling an enormous length of limb, and went over to the door, peeking out into the corridor. "You never know." He closed the door again with care, lowering his voice. "Righto! You know that hung-over Cypress just below the temple turn-off? That's your going point. You plow east there. Right through the brush and mesquite."

"Thank you. You are being very helpful, Mr. O'Flannery."

"Irish."

"Irish . . ." She had started out when her naturally suspicious mind got the better of her and she turned back. "Mr. O'Flannery, aren't you afraid to help someone like me?"

"You bet your best four-in-hand! But old Irish has something going for him that puts him one up on the big shots here."

Kay laughed. "I'm sure you have."

But he seemed serious. "It's just this. I came here because of a female. A bitch if ever there was one—Nadine Janocek! Janos to you. But she's the woman for me, and I stay. I never signed, though. I'm not under contract. I never received any benefits. Any crumbs of so-called happiness I get, I get by old Irish's fatal charm. You'd be surprised how that protects me."

"Can you explain something about the running of this place? What it means about signing leases and contracts and all? *What is going on here?*"

"Sorry." His shake of the head was so firm, so definite it troubled her more than the refusal itself.

Kay took a long, deep breath, looked around the room, noted the elegance, the remnants of delicious food, the soft, Sybaritic quality of the air itself. "Everything most people can possibly want," she remarked, wondering even as she spoke. "Yet I feel as if everything were closing in on me, as if I were in purgatory. Or hell. And never . . . never could get out. Why does it affect me like that, in spite of the elegance?"

"Do get out!" he said roughly, waving one big hand. "Get out now. Tonight. And no more questions."

"Thank you. I will." She opened the door, closed it quietly but with decision, and almost tripped over the little striped tabby cat who sat in the dark hall with his bushy tail wrapped around his paws. She might not have seen him at all but for the feline brightness of his eyes gleaming in the dark.

"Damn it! Will you get out from underfoot!"

She could never remember speaking so abruptly in that querulous tone to a cat or a dog. But Kinkajou's eerie, silent presence now only added to her terrors. She went rapidly out of the Spa.

It was still dusk and the blue mists of twilight were creeping in upon the valley. More than ever she was aware of a dreadful sense of enclosure, of being squeezed in and bound by threads, soft, translucent and deadly as a spider's web. Irish was right. She would leave tonight. At once. But the sense of loss that sent her to Lucifer Cove seeking vengeance was doubled now. Her suspicions of Arthur Dugald, who had been so close to Leo and, indirectly, to Kay herself, were like losing Leo all over again.

She had already started along the street under the overhanging second stories of the Tudor buildings when she heard her name called. She began to run, then turned, saw the blonde young receptionist of the Spa, and retraced her steps.

"Did you call me?"

"Yes, Ma'am. You were at the Hot Springs this afternoon; weren't you?"

Puzzled at the girl's nervousness and anxiety, Kay agreed that she had been at the Hot Springs to see Dr. Rossiter.

"And no one else, Mrs. Aronson?"

"No one." Then Kay amended, "Except Thalia Cates."

"I mean your friend, Mr. Dugald. Did you see him at the Hot Springs?" When Kay shook her head, wondering what this was leading to, the girl went on breathlessly. "But he was coming back here, don't you see? And he didn't come. He's still in there."

Kay was annoyed at her own stab of panic. After all, he was very likely a part of this vicious community! Hadn't Marc Meridon mentioned that Dulane was at Lucifer Cove in some time past? And he had been allowed to leave at that time, probably to work first for the threatened labor leader, Aristede Amanos in Detroit, and then for Leo Aronson.

"I'm sure he knows what he is doing. If I were you, Miss Bryer, I wouldn't worry too much about him. He has a way of landing on his feet."

"But—but—we were joking about the danger there. And it's true. He shouldn't have tried to prowl around in that place. Now, he's gone. It's all wrong. He should've been back long before this. What can we do?"

Kay was torn by conflicting impulses. She would have given much to be able to trust Arthur Dugald. In which case, she would be confronted by the necessity of a monumental rescue operation, and she was not equipped, mentally or physically, to pull off anything like that. On the other hand, since Arthur was a friend of Marc Meridon, any talk about rescue was purely academic.

"My suggestion," she said indifferently, "is to report this to your employer, Mr. Meridon. Let him take over from there. I'm sure he would love to. They are old friends." That sent the girl hurrying back into the Spa, while Kay seized the chance and started down the street again toward the plank bridge. She was running by the time she reached the steadily rising trail. Thankful that she wore the neat but practical boots which made her stiff climb easier, she started upward.

Night came down upon the valley floor with terrifying suddenness, but ahead of her in the upper reaches of the trail Kay could still make out the objects, rocks, trees, winter debris, that lined the trail; for the sky was at least an hour lighter than the ground beneath her feet. She was approaching the cypress that Irish had mentioned when the beseeching branches seemed to take sudden life, and she saw that someone was waiting for her behind the tree.

This latest incursion upon her privacy, her right to do as she chose with her life, was too much to bear. How dare they send some creep up into the darkness to stop her! She clenched her fists, digging her manicured fingernails into her palms, stiffened belligerently, and strode on.

"Mrs. Aronson!" called the silhouetted figure in a woman's voice. "Please—give me a moment."

It was Christine Deeth.

In spite of all her clenched fists and brave intentions, Kay retreated a few steps.

"You—startled me! I'm in a hurry. You want to see me?"

"I want to tell you something, Mrs. Aronson. About your telephone call. I came up to the chalet but Caro said you hadn't returned yet. You did call to Detroit. About one of your husband's employees?"

The woman was probably going to tell her some cock-and-bull story that suited Lucifer Cove for her to know. She played it cool, careful not to say too much.

"I did make a telephone call. It wasn't important. Merely an inquiry about Mr. Dugald's previous . . . associations."

Christine peered around into the darkness nervously. Although Kay could see nothing suspicious around them except the mountainside with its tiny sounds of nature adapting to the night, Christine lowered her voice.

"You did not reach Detroit, Mrs. Aronson."

"Oh, but I did. I talked to the Detroit operator. Mr. Dugald's former employer no longer lives there. As a matter of fact, I have reason to believe he is dead."

Christine Deeth shook her head. "You are only partly right. Mr. Amanos is dead, but you did not speak to the Detroit operator. That was one of the Spa's operators. They monitor calls like yours." Kay gasped, and began to take a sudden, tense interest in the woman. Christine went on. "I made your call myself when I heard what had happened. I am in a unique position for—for private reasons. And I can tell you that whatever suspicions you harbored against Arthur Dugald, they are false. I talked with the Detroit police among others. He did not murder Mr. Amanos. Nor did he attempt to kill him. He is a highly trained agent hired to protect men like your husband and Mr. Amanos. And as a matter of fact, it was he who saved the union leader's life during that attempt seven years ago."

"But Mr. Amanos is dead now."

"Not surprising, Mrs. Aronson. He died last year of arteriosclerosis. He was seventy-eight."

Kay walked on a few yards with her. Bits of shale, slippery and light, slipped away from under her feet, rattling and crackling through thickets as they fell. Both women started uneasily and Kay asked, "How do you know about Arthur? And the attempted assassination of the labor leader?"

"Because the two assassins were clients of the Hot Springs before they went to Detroit to fill what they called their contract."

"You mean, there were people at Lucifer Cove who knew what those killers planned?"

Christine said gently, "You still don't understand. The . . . the management of Lucifer Cove makes no moral judgments." She added with a small, sad smile, "You can verify Mr. Dugald's innocence when you leave here. The Detroit police know the full story."

It was too much for Kay. She gave up her pursuit of what Mrs. Deeth called "moral judgments." Of more immediate importance was the reinstatement of Arthur as a man to trust, a man of quiet strength and superior mentality. And in the train of that realization came the shocking news from Bonnie Lou Bryer.

As the women passed under one of the high, infrequent little electric lights that gave the trail its pattern of black velvet occasionally sprinkled with brilliance, Christine Deeth saw Kay's face and asked quickly.

"What is it? What is wrong?"

"That girl at the reception desk, the little blonde. She was worried about Arthur. Said he should have come back before this."

Christine stopped, staring at her. "Where had he gone?"

"To the Hot Springs. I heard him questioning Miss Bryer about those passages at the Springs, especially the lower areas." When she returned Christine's gaze, she knew they understood each other. Both of them were aware of the eerie danger in the lower regions of the Hot Springs. Kay made the obvious effort. "Mrs. Deeth, couldn't you call the sheriff's office at Santarita, tell them we are in danger?" Her voice trailed off into the tiny night sounds. She said tiredly after a moment, "You can't bring help. You are a part of this horror; aren't you?" It was not necessary for Christine Deeth to answer. The truth was written in her anguished face.

She whispered hoarsely, "You must get him out of there. Wait! I'll find out if he is actually to die tonight. Come. Nadine won't be in the temple yet. We can call from there and check with the records."

"No! I couldn't go in there again. Not after . . . I couldn't!"

"Yes, you can." The frail, delicate woman could be surprisingly firm. "Come along. You are quite safe as long as I am with you."

This was odd. Everything about Christine Deeth's special position here was odd. And then Kay remembered what Caro Teague had said, that the Deeth woman was Marc Meridon's mistress. There seemed no more doubt that attractive, gentle Marc Meridon was the evil genius of Lucifer Cove. It was alarming, but not as bad as the possibility of Arthur Dugald's being guilty. She followed Christine over the westerly path and though she shuddered at the memory of those moments early in the day, she went in after Christine who unlocked the big doors with her own key.

The long auditorium of the temple looked quite different at this hour of the evening. Rows of collapsible chairs had been set up, but Kay ignored these. The place was lit as before by the little blue light with the long chain. She saw now that it cast out many darts of light and was, in fact, a prism, constantly if slightly turning. She looked away in haste, feeling in her vivid imagination the links of that chain cutting into the tender flesh of her throat, cutting her windpipe, choking her.

Recovering after a sudden attack of coughing, she ran after Christine, who was already on the dais and moving through the doorway into the narrow hall behind it. The telephone Christine used was in a stuffy little costume room, thick with dust and body-powder. She spoke to the operator who was probably the Spa receptionist.

"This is Christine Deeth. Will you give me the reception desk on the second floor of the Hot Springs?" She motioned for Kay to come nearer and they listened together to the voice at the other end of the line.

Christine said, "Mrs. Cates? On her relief? Thank you. Who is this?"

A male voice spoke. "This is Guiffredo, Signora. May I be of assistance?"

Christine laughed, a forced, light laugh that Kay suspected was false. "Perhaps you may. I am curious about one of the new clients, an Arthur Dugald. Is he in your white file?"

There was a little pause, some cards riffled, Guiffredo's voice again. "Not the white file, Signora." He hesitated. "I tell you this in confidence. The gentleman's card was moved to the black file some minutes ago."

Staring at Christine, Kay thought her face had

turned ashen, but the woman went on, in a lower voice, carefully excluding emotion.

"Does it say when?"

Guiffredo apparently examined the card. "Tonight, Signora. By twenty-two hours. That is to say, by ten o'clock. There was another first, as you know. The woman Schallert."

Christine set the phone back with her shaking hand. Her eyes were closed. She seemed to be praying, and her despair, her terror conveyed themselves to Kay.

"What did it mean—ten o'clock?"

Christine said, "For disposal. The furnaces at ten."

FOURTEEN

"What do we do first? Tell me. What?"

Christine wavered, leaned against the thick closetful of black penitent robes. "It is too late. When it has gone this far, there is no stopping it. It is beyond human power."

"Don't give me that! Don't talk like that." When Kay was most desperate she was most furious. She took Christine by the shoulder and would have shaken her but for the peculiar, hollow, ringing sound of a gong that made both women look anxiously at the open door. Christine recovered first.

"It is the hourly gong, one of Nadine's sound effects. Believe me Mrs. Aronson, we have tried before, but once the client has signed and bought all that he could possibly wish for except his life, he pays his debt."

"And sometimes they call it suicide!"

Christine nodded wordlessly. She seemed incapable of further movement. Kay looked at her with contempt, then turned and, moving rapidly through the dark auditorium, rushed out across

the portico. Going down the steps she recalled the
.32 automatic at the chalet. At least, she would
not be such a fool as to venture out again without
a weapon, a loaded weapon.

No one was in the chalet, but the living room
and kitchen had been cleaned and dusted. There
was a note from Caro Teague saying that she had
gone down to the Spa for dinner because "being
alone in the chalet makes me nervous."

"Nor can I blame her," Kay told herself vehe-
mently.

She found the automatic, checked the cartridge
clip, and put it into the pocket of her warm, beat-
up vicuna jacket. There were hundreds of things
she ought to do. She studied the telephone for
several seconds, finally picked it up. The first voice
she heard was the night operator at the Spa.
Without speaking, she set the phone back.

It was very well to play the dauntless deliverer
in front of Christine Deeth, but it was a long way
from the chalet to the lower depths of the Hot
Springs, long in every sense, because there was
going to be a great deal more to a rescue than
just scaring the inhabitants of the Hot Springs
with a bullet or two.

Would a bullet actually frighten them, those
peculiar, wrinkle-free and coldly handsome zombies who worked at the Hot Springs?

It was after seven. Better stop arguing the
matter or the whole ghastly business would be
completed, and without even the threat of a bullet. She left the chalet, remembered too late that
she had forgotten to lock the door, and then
shrugged and went on. As she reached the temple,

Christine Deeth came hurrying out as if she had been lying in wait to pounce onto Kay.

Kay was unnerved by the suddenness of the woman's appearance, her fine-spun golden hair wild around her face, her features as distraught as Kay felt.

"Mrs. Aronson! I can't let you go there without help. Come along. Do you have a flash, in case?"

Kay felt in the pocket of her after-ski pants. "I've the little hand light. Hurry!"

Already, there were furtive groups of Nadine's followers making their way up the trail toward the devil's temple and the night service. The singles marched up uneasily, casting quick glances at passersby, assessing the possibilities. Most of the pairs were young and heterosexual, hugging each other for courage. Christine ignored them all. It was as if she had become so used to this strange nether-world that she no longer saw them at all. Kay was aware of passersby but only as obstacles in her frantic hurry.

The plank bridge was so jammed with devil-worshippers and curiosity-seekers that neither woman recognized Irish O'Flannery and the small woman beside him, her head dark and sleek, staring through smoky blue eyes at Christine and Kay. Irish called, waved to the two women and strode on up the mountain trail with Nadine.

"What on earth does he see in her?" Kay asked, looking back once.

Christine smiled faintly but made no judgment on the matter.

Once they reached the village main street Christine showed Kay the quicker route to the Hot

202

Springs behind the long series of Tudor buildings. It was dry, bumpy desert ground, but neither the mesquite bushes nor the yellow curls of sulphur seeping through the earth's crust stopped the two women.

"The back way is best," Christine said, pointing east of the Hot Springs complex. "Through the burned area. Incidentally, Nadine isn't all bad, you know. My little son was visiting me last summer and Nadine risked her life to save him in the fire."

Christine might feel gratitude to the priestess but this had no effect on Kay, who still remembered with a tight throat the hypnotic effect of the devil's temple. She followed Christine around the far east walls of the sprawling complex, and they entered through a patio whose fence had partially burned. Wild flowers were sticking up bravely in the dirt all around the unidentifiable crushed stone figure in the center of a dry fountain.

"There really is life, of sorts, here, after all," Kay reflected as they abruptly entered a hall whose outside door into the patio had been burned off and the debris removed. In spite of that removal, entering the Hot Springs clinic and disposal area at this ground floor level was like entering an inferno on the Night After. There had been tiny lights, like fireflies in a partially burned oak tree that spread across one corner of the patio, but inside the Hot Springs complex there were only the high, dim, concealed neon lights that made everything including the faces of the woman look milky blue, like recently dead flesh.

"Do you know where this leads to?" Kay whispered, but Christine waved her to silence.

They had passed their first door on the right and Christine opened it onto the landing of a metal staircase that led both upward and down, when Kay was jolted by Christine's violent, backward step. She seemed stupefied with shock, and Kay pushed past her, starting up the stairs.

Seated at the top of the flight was the ubiquitous Kinkajou. If a cat could be said to smile, the little striped tabby did so. Kay felt the reverberations of the shock that seemed to have rendered Christine dumb and motionless, and the only possible explanation could be some sort of phobia Christine had against cats. And even that did not take into consideration the ring she wore.

Having passed the cat, who made no attempt to interfere, Kay opened the door at the top of the steps and it slammed shut behind her. She did not hear Christine following and gave the woman up. She found, however, that she had come out on the second floor, very close to the desk where the hairdresser, Guiffredo, sat, still on what was probably Thalia Cates' dinner relief. He looked absolutely horrified at sight of her, and got up in such a hurry his chair fell over with a crash against one of the white and gold file cabinets.

"Signora Aronson! You are not to be here without escort. My regrets, but . . ."

"Don't be ridiculous!" she dismissed him briskly with an ease that was entirely fictitious. Audacity and an assumption of authority were her best weapons here. "Mr. Meridon sent me to check a—a mistake in the manifest."

Obviously, the hairdresser had never been to

sea. He didn't understand her and was not quite sure enough of his own position to argue with her. She was glad of that. She had slowed her rapid pace but managed to look properly authoritarian as she passed him and went down the passage with the grey arrows, past Dr. Rossiter's closed office. There was a light under the office door. She had no time to wonder whether Clive Rossiter was there or not.

Her heartbeat seemed to increase, but her terror was reduced by the firm resolve to fight it out now that the danger was so close. Around the corner of the passage was the door to the staircase, and halfway down, the little room where Edna Schallert's body had been readied for the disposal units.

The door was ajar, Kay slipped in. The single, high, swinging little globe was so dim she could hardly make out any difference between her shocking discovery of Edna Schallert earlier in the day and the same sheeted and shrouded figure on the wheeled metal table before her now. Puzzled, she reached for the sheet, angry at her fingers that trembled as they pulled it away from the shroud. Here was the red plastic tag hung over the shrouded figure, drawn in around the neck. She turned up the tag with thumb and forefinger to catch the light and read what she dreaded:

ARTHUR ADAM DUGALD
#2620-71-71
NO OUTSIDE CONNECTIONS
FOR IMMEDIATE DISPOSAL

She had been terrified at this confirmation of all her worst fears, but now that it had happened she found herself burning with fury. She knew why Arthur had come here and risked his life. His motive was exactly the same as her own. She had been nearly as close to him as to Leo in the past five years. To lose Arthur now was to lose herself, and Leo! She began to tear away the carelessly handsewn shroud with her fingernails. During these few seconds she had resigned herself to the discovery that he was dead. But suddenly, as the heavy silk was peeled away from his bloodless face, he groaned.

She stared at the still features. He had not moved. He didn't seem to breathe. There was no sign of a pulse in his throat. In a gingerly way, hardly daring to hope, she touched his cheek. Cool. But not cold, she thought. Not dead flesh, thank God! She shook him a little, slapped his cheek very lightly, whispered his name.

"May I ask what you are doing, Mrs. Aronson?"

It was like an icy shower at her back. But before she turned around she had enough presence of mind to drop her hand to her pocket where the automatic weighted it down.

Dr. Clive Rossiter was standing in the doorway, sufficiently blocking her escape without presenting anything more sinister than a slight, perplexed frown and his deep-set, observant eyes.

She decided to brave it. It was even possible that he might be moved either by the gun or the gun backed up by her vehement threats. "This man isn't dead. I don't suppose you examined him before consigning him to what we might call . . . the pits of hell."

"Rather melodramatic, Mrs. Aronson." But she thought she had startled him. He took a step toward her.

She indicated her pocket. "I'm afraid I'll have to add another bit of melodrama. I'm armed. Don't come too close to me. But you can do me a favor. Bring Mr. Dugald around. Now!"

"Mr. Dugald! You must be mistaken. He signed nothing. He was not to die."

"Then how do you explain this?"

She moved back into a corner beyond the head of the table, raising her hand far enough so that he could see she was not bluffing about her weapon. He glanced at it, but only in passing, as if it were of no importance. His chief concern was the unconscious man, which rather surprised her and threw her off her stride. She had supposed he was just another in this nasty clutch of fiends, but he was now working very hard to bring Arthur Dugald back to consciousness. His thin, capable thumbs, somewhere in the vicinity of Arthur's jugular vein and at the nape of his neck, had their effect.

In a few minutes, Arthur was actually awake, looking up quizzically at the doctor and then at Kay. With the doctor's help he sat up, grimaced, muttered thickly, "What a head! That Guiffredo must have been carrying a pile-driver."

Kay couldn't help saying, "Thank you, Dr. Rossiter. You seem to be the only honest man in this horrible place."

But he wasn't moved by her apology and compliment. "Not at all, Mrs. Aronson. It is only that there are rules. Even where I—work. Someone wanted Mr. Dugald destroyed, against all our policies. But I could not permit that unless he had signed the lease. It is quite beyond the agreement between me and the—the management." He talked in riddles, and she was in a great hurry. While he was ripping the threads of the shroud, Kay said,

"If you aren't in this plot, Doctor, can you show us how to get out of here? I know what to do about the caves, the way to the next valley, but we've got to get that far. Are you able to walk, Arthur?"

"Believe me, anything is better than being burned alive." He laughed without much humor. "I was having nightmares. I dreamed I had died." Dr. Rossiter and Kay looked at each other. Dugald caught the exchange. "Or is this what they call a living nightmare?" He began to kick off the remnants of the shroud, stopped to finger the back of his head and to wince painfully. "I imagine it is too much to ask that one of you has a couple of aspirin." In spite of the scarcity of aspirin, however, he was on his feet by this time with scarcely more than a tremor.

Dr. Rossiter had gone to the door, looked out. "You are safe for the moment. Can you walk the distance? I'll give you a few bits of advice. I doubt if this will help you, but try not to be seen. Try not to leave a trail. Try to avoid all animals. Human or otherwise."

. . . Especially cats, thought Kay. Yes, Kinkajou was in this somewhere. And less than half an hour ago the innocent-looking little cat had been separated from this room by hardly more than one wall.

Arthur Dugald appreciated the necessity for haste. He was on his feet and ready to leave by the time Kay joined him. Dr. Rossiter motioned them out onto the landing and when they would have gone down the steps, he indicated the opposite direction.

They started along the upper hall. By the time they reached the far end of the hall and another flight of steps, Dugald was nearly his old capable self.

"You must have a cast-iron head," Kay remarked in admiration.

He agreed with dry amusement, "It used to be my stock in trade, that and my highly forgettable face."

They raced down the stairs. At the bottom, beyond a narrow foyer, was the north end of the burned out patio. They crossed it sedately, in case any pairs who had sought the darkness should notice them, but beyond the walls of the Hot Springs Dugald was making time like an experienced long distance runner. It was all Kay could do to keep up with him.

"I think we'll be all right now," she told him breathlessly. "All the troublemakers were at the Hot Springs."

By the time they reached the plank bridge below the trail, it looked as though the nightmare might be ending. The night had turned out clear and crisp. The low, hanging sky was full of stars.

"Just where do we find those caves of yours?" Dugald asked, only a trifle winded.

She leaned against the cypress, gasping, rubbing her side, hoping the painful stitch would go away.

"Starting here. You know, Arthur, this is the first time you've ever sounded like a plain, ordinary human being, and not Leo's secretary."

He smiled. "Getting one's head bashed in and enjoying a shrouded sleep does wonders in reducing things to bare essentials."

He looked away, frowning. "I failed with Aronson. I asked him not to go without me, or some other protection. But of course—" he looked back at her, "—he had no choice. He had to come. Like those others here, he made a deal. Long ago he signed the lease. Whatever it is. And the moment came when payment was demanded."

She only half understood him and did not want to understand him fully. "Are you OK? I'm ready."

He took her arm as if she were the one who needed help, and they made their way east from the cypress across a narrow gulley to the slope of the eastern range. In a matter of minutes they could see the cave opening, its dark mouth outlined by the starlight.

"I can't believe it," she murmured, breathing deeply as they made their way over the debris at the entrance. It had been washed there by the last flash flood and they could hear the crunch of their own footsteps as they entered, finding it necessary to stoop under the low, dripping roof after they crossed the wide entrance. The immediate cave they had penetrated was soon elongated into a tunnel with an uncomfortably low and rocky roof.

Kay gave her tiny flashlight to Dugald. "It's atomic or something, and supposed to last a lifetime. Whether yours or mine, they didn't say.

Keep your finger constantly on the little round button."

For a few minutes their footsteps on the wet pebbles and sand, combined with the noisy echo from each drop of water effectively deafened them to any other sounds. But when they reached a point in the mountain where the roof was over six feet above them, they stopped to straighten and stretch, massaging each other's painful shoulders. Kay was feeling proud of herself and relieved over Dugald's iron constitution, but one sight of his tense, listening features in the tiny radius of light sent her back into her old terrors.

"What is it?" she whispered before he motioned her to silence. He shut off the light at the same time. It was hard for her to make out distinct sounds over the steady drip-drip from some crevice overhead, but there was certainly a small light moving somewhere behind them, and now she could make out the crackle of other boots moving over the rocky surface. The cave broke up just beyond her and Dugald, into another low-roofed tunnel, and when he nudged her she hurried on, her eyes making out a trail by the faint glow of their pursuer's light. Whoever it was, he had not yet realized their own light was off and that he was betraying his presence.

Kay silently passed the automatic to Dugald who kept it in his free left hand as they moved on. He dropped behind her a few feet, and when he approached again, he whispered, "Guiffredo." She was considerably relieved. The hairdresser hardly sent her into a paroxysm of fright. At his gesture she hurried on, slipping several times on the wet sand in the little runnels along the lower wall.

She was now properly bruised, with numerous pulled muscles, but she felt nothing except the passionate urge to keep moving.

Again, Dugald fell behind. She looked back. He had pressed hard against the wall, hidden from view of their pursuer around a sharp, jutting core of rock. She looked back just in time to see the edge of Dugald's hand chop viciously across the wrist of the hairdresser who groaned, knocked breathless by the pain, and fell to his knees. The flashlight and a heavy, flat-looking automatic rolled over the ground toward Kay. She picked both up with shaking fingers. In those few seconds the thought flashed through her brain: "It's all over. We're home safe."

She had just taken a step forward, hearing Dugald urge Guiffredo in front of him when the cave, the endless dark ahead, even the walls and the dripping roof, reverberated with the ghastly baying of a hound. Kay fell back, cracking her head painfully against the wall. She knew the source of the noise. The pale, liver-colored hound. That very presentiment of death. She looked around. Arthur had recovered first and was nudging Guiffredo. The latter looked stupefied. He was crouching, with his hands over his ears. Dugald, catching Kay's shocked gaze, shook his head. He stepped around Guiffredo, motioning Kay ahead. She was rapidly learning to trust his orders.

"Don't think about it. A hound is only a hound," he said as he reached her.

She reacted to his quiet confidence as much as to his order, and when the baying sound began its horrible arc again, she hurried on under his influence, with the conviction that if Leo had listened to Arthur Dugald, he might be alive today. The roof of the tunnel began to slope upward. They were coming to another cave, surely the last, opening out upon the next valley and away from the madness of Lucifer Cove. Kay began to say, "We've done it!"

At the same time that she slipped into the larger room of the cave, a shadow crossed her face and she closed her eyes, opening them to see what had blinded her momentarily. It was Marc Meridon who had come between her and the bright, full moonlight of the cave exit behind him. She saw him then as she had always seen him, slim and pallid, the least harmful of men, with his somber dark eyes and his wistful smile that twisted her heart a little, even now.

"Mrs. Aronson, you are surprisingly troublesome."

Speechless, Kay made vague motions with Guiffredo's heavy automatic whose working she devoutly hoped was the same as her own thirty-two. How did you free the safety catch? . . . But the Spa's manager did not move. There seemed to be no bluffing him. She raised the gun.

Behind her, Arthur Dugald said, "Don't argue. Pass him." He had the shaking, moaning Guiffredo under one arm, and was half-carrying him along.

Following Dugald's orders Kay took several halting steps before another of those ghastly howls stopped her abruptly. Although Marc Meridon had made no move, he was obviously aware of the liver-colored hound slinking silently into the cave, his form etched by the bright, rising moon behind him.

Shuddering, Kay stared at the hound, fascinated by the eyes, the color of pale mud. She saw the great canine teeth bared, the bones move under the sleek skin. The creature was gathering his muscles for a spring. At the same time Dugald moved past her, within a foot of Marc. She cried out, expecting to see him crushed by the hound, but Dugald had moved so unexpectedly the hound's leap carried him to the wretched Guiffredo. Dugald grasped at Marc's shoulder, as if for support, and Kay rushed past him to the cave entrance. There she dared to look back.

Arthur had taken hold of the red scarf Marc wore, and dragged it off. Terrified, Kay cried, "Arthur! Run!" but became aware that Marc had made no effort to seize him. As Arthur pointed a long arm at Marc Meridon's bare throat, Marc merely shrugged and flipped a casual little salute to them.

Kay stared unbelieving, in horror. The pale flesh of Marc's throat was a gaping, torn wound, only just beginning to heal. And still he smiled, his eyebrows raised slightly in that satiric way of his. She turned, stumbling blindly out into the sweet, clean air.

Guiffredo's screams tore the night but there was no sound from the great hound. Kay turned back, unable to bear the dying man's cries. But the sounds had stopped and a few minutes later Arthur Dugald joined her and they began the stiff descent to a valley town so normal, with its neat strings of night lights, and its open fields for milk cattle, that Kay was weeping with relief when Arthur said finally,

"We've made it. It's over, Kay. No crying now.

My brave girl." His arm strengthened as his words warmed her.

They stopped on the highway into the town. Both looked back up the mountain which was now heavily shrouded in darkness as the moon moved overhead. Kay tried to speak, managed finally, "Why?"

"You mean, why didn't he destroy us? I don't believe it is Meridon's way. His victims destroy themselves."

"No, no. The hound. He is Marc's enemy. I saw them fight once. A deadly dog and—and cat fight."

She thought he was going to avoid the terrible question, but he said after a little pause, "I don't think they are enemies . . . You might think of them as the devil and death."

"But they quarreled once. I saw them."

"Isn't it possible that death wished to take something that belonged to . . . Marc?"

"Christine Deeth?" Very likely, she thought, and then groaned as she tried to reason out the nightmare of the last few days. "If all this is true, then the hound did not pursue us because it already had a victim. Guiffredo." In the distance, as in all highly respectable California towns, they saw the flagpole, and the signs of the California Patrol office. "We must report the whole thing to the police. Have them raid the Cove."

"Can we?"

She looked at him and belatedly understood. "There will be nothing. As there was nothing I could prove about Leo's death. He and his pilot took the plane up. It crashed. Leo died. And all the inquests and all the investigations in the world won't change it. Only you and I know why he left the Cove in that hurry."

He said in a sudden access of anger, "And we can't prove it!"

They walked in silence until, as if with an identical impulse, they reached for each other's hand and entered the highly civilized little town which, in its civilized way, had pulled in the sidewalks at ten o'clock.

Civilized or not, it too feared the demons of night.

Another tumultuous romantic novel
by Patricia Matthews,
author of the multi-million
copy national bestseller,
LOVE'S AVENGING HEART

Love's Wildest Promise

P40-047 $1.95

Sarah Moody was a lady's maid in a wealthy London home. But suddenly her quiet sheltered world was turned upside down when she was abducted and smuggled aboard a ship bound for the colonies. Its cargo—whores to satisfy the appetites of King George's soldiers in New York. Was Sarah destined to become one of these women? Or would she find the man she was searching for, the man who would help her to fulfill Love's Wildest Promise.

If you can't find this book at your local bookstore, simply send the cover price, plus 25¢ for postage and handling to:

 Pinnacle Books
Reader Mailing Service, P.O. Box 1050,
Rockville Centre, N.Y. 11571

The epic novel of the Old South,
ablaze with the unbridled passions
of men and women seeking
new heights for their love

Windhaven Plantation

Marie de Jourlet

P40-022 $1.95

Here is the proud and passionate story of one man—
Lucien Bouchard. The second son of a French nobleman,
a man of vision and of courage, Lucien dares to seek a new
way of life in the New World that suits his own high
ideals. Yet his true romantic nature is at war with his
lusty, carnal desires. The four women in his life reflect
this raging conflict: Edmée, the high-born, amoral
French sophisticate who scorns his love, choosing his
elder brother, heir to the family title; Dimarte, the in-
genuous, earthy, and sensual Indian princess; Amelia,
the fiery free-spoken beauty who is trapped in a life of
servitude for crimes she didn't commit; and Priscilla,
whose proper manner hid the unbridled passion of her
true desires.

"... will satisfy avid fans of the plantation genre."
—*Bestsellers* magazine

If you can't find this book at your local bookstore, simply
send the cover price plus 25¢ for postage and handling to

 Pinnacle Books
275 Madison Avenue, New York, New York 10016

PH-15